PRAISE FOR
Breaking Out

"A harrowing incident involving her talented teenage son helps dermatologist Susannah realize she has kept herself from moving forward after the death of her beloved husband, Stan. At times humorous, at other times poignant, *Breaking Out* is an eloquent exploration of how difficult life can be following the unexpected death of a loved one. With a wealth of detail, including the complexities of family relationships, Mary Flinn creates a heartwarming story about the curious way two people can connect through grief and break out into a new life together."

— Jane Tesh, author of the *Madeline Maclin Mysteries*
and *The Grace Street Series*

"With *Breaking Out*, Mary Flinn hits her stride in creating realistic romantic situations filled with all the emotional baggage and quirks we all bring to them. Main character Susannah Brody endears herself to readers because she is so very much like all of us, wanting and needing love, but unsure how to acquire it. And that's all the more reason why we cheer her on."

— Tyler Tichelaar, Ph.D., and award-winning author of
Arthur's Legacy and *The Best Place*

"Will redemption be able to rise in crescendo above layers of heartbreak? Award-winning author Mary Flinn deserves a standing ovation for her composition of lies, loss, and hope played magnificently by finely tuned characters in *Breaking Out*. In this novel, a small-town widowed dermatologist faces an approaching empty nest as her college-bound son prepares for a music camp—the last of the summer—before he heads off to college. Her memories of life with her husband and her internal dialog with him have kept her tempo steady for several years now, yet when her son goes missing, the strong bond she's always felt with her deceased husband seems to have gone missing, too. Susannah must trust a local police detective to help her find her son...and her faith in the possibility of love. With her sixth novel, Flinn continues to orchestrate touching stories that inspire and remind us that love is possible, no matter the circumstances."

— Laura Wharton, award-winning author of
The Pirate's Bastard and *Leaving Lukens*
and books for children

"Mary Flinn's *Breaking Out* is a simultaneously poignant and funny story about the hold our past has on us, even when we yearn to embrace the changes that shape our future. Flinn beautifully reminds us that we all share the trials and triumphs of family, friendships, and neighbors, and we all relate to her story because we share being human."

— Sabrina Stephens, author of
Banker's Trust and *Canned Good*

To LaSandra,

BREAKING
OUT

A Novel

Follow your dreams!

♥

Mary Flinn

MARY FLINN

Address all inquiries to:
Mary Flinn
mflinn@triad.rr.com
www.TheOneNovel.com

ISBN: 978-0-9907197-0-0

Editor & Proofreader: Tyler R. Tichelaar, Ph.D.
Cover Photo: Mary Flinn
Cover Design/Interior Layout: Fusion Creative Works, www.fusioncw.com

Printed in the United States of America
Published by Fiction Worx

First Printing 2014

For additional copies, visit: www.TheOneNovel.com

To forever friends: Anne and Mimi

ACKNOWLEDGMENTS

Being a novelist can be a lonely vocation. In the creation of *Breaking Out*, as with all my work, I have found camaraderie in researching a certain aspect of the story, or in bouncing ideas off my friends who are willing to listen to me and share in my imaginary life, encouraging the muse and cheering me on. Thanks to Mimi Williams, Laura Wharton, and Jane Tesh for being actively interested and lifting me up when I needed it.

Thanks to my family: my husband, Mike Flinn, has little choice but to indulge my fantasies, but he is always there (usually after dinner when I've plied him with alcohol and am holding him hostage), listening to my ideas, making (great) suggestions, making me laugh, feeding me, and telling me never to give up. To my daughters, Jessica and Shelby, although you are far away, you are both still close in my heart. Thanks to all of you for your support, ideas, and most of all, your love!

Several people have helped answer my questions along this journey. I owe a great deal of gratitude (that I can only repay in the form of a free book!) to Dr. Laura Lomax and Dr. Karol Wolicki for answering my medical questions. Gail F. Hutchison, Victim's Advocate, and her detective friends in Dare County were instrumental in the development of my detective's work. Michelle Cone was kind enough to help me pin down some of the musical details of several of the pieces mentioned in the story, in addition to pouring my wine and promoting my work at Stonefield Cellars Winery in Stokesdale, North Carolina. If you are in the area, visit Robert and Natalie Wurz, the owners, and Michelle. You will have a great time.

I am also grateful to Dan Jones, Kim Pendry, and fellow North Carolina authors, Sabrina Stephens, Laura S. Wharton and Jane Tesh for reading my manuscript and giving me positive feedback. I know how busy you all are, and it humbles me to know you have neglected something important just to assist me.

Breaking Out would not be as beautiful as it is without the creative genius of Shiloh Schroeder of Fusion Creative Works. Dr. Tyler R. Tichelaar is still a prince, without whose editing prowess I would have a merely mediocre novel. Thanks for pushing me to take Susannah and Chase to the next level. You two are my dream team!

And finally, a huge thank you goes out to my readers. Many of you are still hanging on, which I appreciate more than you could possibly know. To those who have posted reviews, you are the best! Without my readers, I would have thrown in the towel long ago; writing is no way to make a living—that is without that coveted movie deal or a spot on the *New York Times* Bestseller list. One can still hope, but I thrive on hearing that question that so many of you ask: "When is your next book coming out?" As long as you are reading them, I will continue to write them. I'm eternally grateful for you!

Chapter 1

STAN DAY

It's been three years. I push my nose into the soft collar of Stan's navy plaid bathrobe, the one I gave him for Christmas the first year we were married, and breathe in his scent; the scent takes me back to him instantly, the way a smell can catapult a memory to the forefront of one's mind in a nanosecond, like nothing else can. As I stand in his closet, breathing in his memories, running my hand along his dress shirts, his ties, the pairs of slacks in varied shades of three colors—black, gray, and khaki—I can feel his presence, still. His is a small collection of clothing for such a grand person, yet I can't bring myself to part with any of it. It is only in these rare times when I'm alone that I indulge myself in such a seemingly small comfort, but for me, it is huge. He is here.

Stan Brody would be shaking his head if he could see me now (and I believe he can). So would my eighteen-year-old son, Myers, who will be coming home from a camping trip with his father within the hour. I've already had my morning run and shower, so I will indulge myself with a cup of coffee, shamelessly wear Stan's robe, and spend a few idle moments on my porch, the way most of us do in Magnolia Village on Saturday mornings. I wander out and take my place in my favorite spot on this lovely June morning.

The summer heat will soon begin to creep up as the accompanying humidity will stretch its fingers up the back of my neck and under my hair. In the heat I won't be able to tolerate the robe for long, and since I want to keep it smelling like Stan and not like me, I only wear it for short periods of time on the anniversary of his death. Seated inconspicuously on my porch swing and shielded from view by passersby on the village green by my spectacular blue hydrangea bush, I swing and sip, eavesdropping on the songbirds that live in my flora. Apart from their cheerful, chirpy gossip, it is quiet at this time of the morning. Only my fellow joggers are out at seven-thirty on a Saturday. I would normally be sleeping in myself, but this morning was one of those times when I jolted awake before dawn and couldn't go back to sleep. *Three years.*

As I expect, I hear the rhythmic pounding of running shoes on cement; it has to be Chase. He runs faster than most, and as usual, I could set my watch by him. I know this from seeing him on school mornings when I'd walk out the door with Myers, to meet up with his friend, Tim, around the block from us, during the days when they'd walked to elementary school together. Chase is unrelenting in his regularity; he is only thwarted if there is a deluge or the occasional icy sidewalk to prevent him from his morning ritual, but in our South Carolina border town, we don't get much ice or snow.

Lieutenant Andrew Chase. It's been almost two years for him. He doesn't see me, but I can see him through the hydrangea leaves, solid and fit in his usual gray T-shirt and shorts, his close-cropped gingery hair just visible through the foliage as he runs effortlessly by my house. I wonder who else I miss on a daily basis when I'm at the office and not on my beloved front porch. Everyone runs by my house since I live across from the park, which is the place to be for exercise and fellowship with the neighbors. I love this street. When Stan and I looked for houses, it reminded me of my old restored Victorian house in the Fourth Ward in Charlotte, where I lived ten years ago, before I married him and Myers and I moved here with him. Slipping just over the North Carolina state line, many of us transplants have chosen to live in our village to be close to our jobs in Charlotte, while paying lower taxes in South Carolina. Stan and I wanted a community that was quaint and small, and a new house, with little upkeep since both of us were busy doctors. It needed to be in a neighborhood where convenience and community were priorities, along with charming front porches, a good school, and safe streets. And now, ten years later with Detective Chase pounding the pavement every morning, I definitely feel safe here.

The coffee is rich and warm with just the right amount of cream and sugar. Raw sugar, not the substitute, and just a little. It won't kill me…. I close my eyes and enjoy the nutty aroma that comforts me, along with the feel of Stan's robe. I can almost hear him talking to me in his lilting, New Zealand accent, *Can I pour you a warmer-upper, love? How was your run, Susannah?*

I do this regularly, listening to my deceased husband when I have alone time. I don't think it's creepy, but it's not a pastime I can discuss with many people, only with those few who know me well enough to understand me, whose eyebrows don't ratchet up in fear, revulsion, or skepticism. It would seem to others a pastime uncharacteristic of my scientific nature, indulging myself in the highly spiritual, but I have always believed there is much more to the balance of our lives than only science presents. However weird it is, I try not be sad anymore, just appreciative that Stan was a miracle in my life for the short time I had him. I can't help but cling to the memories of his arms around me, imagining the touch of his fingers on my cheek, trying to feel his kiss and missing him still.

Feeling inside the robe's pocket, I discover that I left his picture in it last year, a shot of him that I took on one of our trips out west with Myers. It's not as though I could ever forget what Stan looked like, but I still love to look at his pictures. There are pictures of him in our house, of course, but maybe I was interrupted last year so I left this one here. On this particular day, June 16th, every year, I pay homage to him by wearing his robe. I look again at Stan's profile, as he looked at Myers, just before turning toward my camera, their faces sharply delineated in the foreground, the Grand Canyon behind them. The moment had been magnificent, and it was one of those times in your life you will always remember with clarity and awe, and treasure for the people with whom you shared it. And Stan had looked magnificent as well, his skin nut-brown from our two-week vacation, the lines around his eyes giving him that character that improves men but that women disdain for themselves. His shock of sandy hair was windblown and longer than he usually wore it. Life as an emergency room doctor left him little time for haircuts or even showers some days. And there was that satisfied grin on his finely chiseled face, as if he were utterly and completely happy with the world at that moment, and I believe he truly was.

Looking at his face in the picture, I can hear his laughter, even though I can't recall exactly what made us laugh other than joy, but nonetheless, the sound rings out so clearly, as if he is still here. I do remember that we all were exuberantly happy on that last vacation with him. The three of us were a family, as much of a family as I could have ever hoped for. The joy from the memory fills me with the same warmth as the coffee, and I know it is him again, telling me not to be sad, not to miss him. *I'm here, Susannah. I'm always here. As long as you love me, I'm here.*

I push the swing with my foot as the birds flutter and call to one another. Someone is building a nest, I see, as a wren makes repeated trips to my window box, pulling threads of moss from my décor to add to hers. My coffee is gone, and as I stand to refill my cup, I reach up to check my hair—dark curls which fall in layers between my cheekbones and the base of my neck; it's almost dry.

As I saunter aimlessly back inside, my cell phone on the kitchen counter rings. It should be Myers, letting me know they are on their way, but it is my father. He and my mother are flying out later this morning on a trip to China with some of their friends so he must be calling to tell me goodbye.

"Hi, Dandy," I say warmly into the phone, using the name that Sloan, my niece had assigned him as a baby. My sister and I thought our children would use Granddad and Grandma as names, but we should have known the task would not be left up to us. It is usually the grandchildren who end up naming the grandparents, giving them the names that stick. So Dandy and Mima, or "Meems," as Myers has further taken it, they are.

"Hello, darling. How are you doing today?" he asks, in that commiserating tone that lets me know he is well aware of the significance of today, and how I'm feeling.

"Oh, I'm okay. I was up really early and went for a run. Couldn't sleep, you know."

"Oh, I'm sure of that. Mima and I still miss Stan, too. It seems it was just yesterday...."

"I know.... So what time are you two heading to the airport?"

"Jen's running us over in about an hour. I'm going to drop Howard at the kennel, but on the way, I wanted to drop off a couple of things—something for you, and something for Myers before he goes to the chamber music camp today. I wanted to see whether you'd be up. I'm two minutes from your house."

"Sure, stop by. I can give you a cup of coffee if you can stay a minute."

"Just for a minute, but no more coffee for me, thank you. I'll see you in just a bit then. Bye!"

"Bye, Dad," I end the call, smiling. My father is the best. I scan the kitchen quickly for any wreckage I'll need to clean up. There is no mess since Myers has gone camping with his father, and I've been here by myself. I have gotten past the irritating habit of letting stacks of mail accumulate on the kitchen counter, forcing myself to deal with it each day the way Stan did. He was enormously tidy. *Handle each piece of paper one time,* was one of his sayings. So I've made myself open the mail, shred it if not needed, or file it away for its proper purpose, and voila! Clean countertop at the end of each day.

"Thank you, baby," I murmur, hugging myself, glad that Stan's good organizational habits have rubbed off on me. I pour myself another cup of coffee as I hear Dad's vintage roadster putter around the corner. He will park as usual at the curb in front of my house. Since I'm still not properly dressed for public display, I will wait for him to come up the stairs. Seeing him pull the candy apple red convertible to the curb, his Panama hat perched jauntily on his head, and Howard, their eleven-year-old golden retriever, riding shotgun in the passenger seat, makes me grin. What a sight they are—two old guys out for a spin on a top-down morning in Magnolia Village!

"Hey, Dad!"

"Hellooo!" he calls, opening his door, and for a man of seventy-eight, emerging surprisingly quickly from the driver's seat. I find myself smiling as he holds open the door, allowing Howard to follow suit. Then he reaches behind the seat, producing a fine black dress shirt on a hanger, covered with a plastic wrapper, and a smaller package. He carries them up the steps to give me a hug. We have the same tall, rakish build, only coincidentally, since I am adopted. Still, my father and I have been linked dramatically since he and my mother chose to start their family by adopting my sister and me. They have always treated us with delighted awe, as if we were some kind of miraculous experiment that they were blessed to stumble upon. But Jen and I were the blessed ones. Being a mother myself, I share those kinds of feelings, but perhaps for different reasons. I am sometimes amazed when others take for granted their own family ties.

"Hey there!" He releases me and I lean down to give Howard's golden head a rub, which makes his plumy tail swing slowly back and forth. He sniffs Stan's robe.

"Good to see you, sweetheart! This is from Mima and me for you," he says, handing me a flat, square package wrapped in colorful paper and tied with raffia—a book, no doubt. We all love to read.

"Thank you!" I say, fingering the simple raffia bow my mother has tied on butterfly paper; it all makes up my favorite kind of package.

"Open it later when you're by yourself. And this is from Mima for Myers."

"Oh, sharp! Look at this! He'll really like this shirt. How'd she know he likes black?"

"She's a bit sharp herself. And look, it has cufflinks, for his performances at the School of the Arts."

Reaching underneath the plastic, I lift a cuff and inspect one of the silver cufflinks in the shape of a violin.

"Now that is a first class gift. He'll be thrilled! I'll have him give Mima a call when he gets home. Hopefully, he'll be able to reach you all before you take off. Please tell her thank you from me, too! What a nice and thoughtful gift! She is so sweet!" I take the shirt and hold it out to look over it again. Myers will love it. He will be one of the few boys to wear a black shirt. Most of them opt for the classic white shirt and black trousers for their concerts, but not my Myers. He's a bit of a rebel. Even his music is unconventional.

Now my dad has noticed what I'm wearing. He clicks his tongue and pushes up his glasses. "Oh...this is Stan's robe!"

I shrug, a bit apologetically. "Yeah, do you think it's weird that I'm wearing it? Like a baby blanket I can't let go of...."

His lips press into a smile that sends me all his empathy. "No, I don't. And it looks great on you, too. If it makes you feel better, then wear it," he says with a swat of his hand. "You'll be okay while we're gone?"

"Of course. Kent is bringing Myers home in just a little while, and then Maggie and Casey are coming by to pick us up about ten o'clock. We'll drive up to Winston-Salem and have lunch, then drop them off at the School of the Arts. Maggie and I are going to spend the night, so you know what that means...."

"Girls' night? Another adventure?"

"Yes, sir! Some shopping, maybe some sightseeing at Reynolda House and Old Salem, and then dinner. You know, she's trying to divert me...."

"Of course, that's what best friends do!"

"I know; she's really great to me, and Casey is so good for Myers, but he hasn't seen her in over two weeks. She's been away at a drama camp."

"What a talent she has! What has she been in lately?"

"Oh, Maggie has a real dilemma! Casey had the lead in *Hairspray*. And she was fantastic from what I heard! Maggie and Ed didn't like the fact that their daughter was so good at it, though! There may be no stopping her from pursuing a musical theater degree now."

"I thought her father wanted her to choose piano."

"Right, or cello—anything but acting." My father and all our friends know that Casey French is a virtuoso pianist and cellist, and since her father was her piano teacher for twelve years, Ed has always hoped she would follow the concert pianist route with her career.

"Well, it's marvelous that she's so talented. I'm sure she'll excel at whatever she chooses." Even after Casey's recent brush with the law, my father has continued to support her, along with Myers, of course, in their music for so many years. A wrong choice resulting in a misdemeanor drug charge for possession of marijuana put an end to Casey's scholarship to the Juilliard School, but she is slated to attend the University of South Carolina in the fall. She is the third of the French children to be in college at the same time, so Maggie and Ed, who live on a tight budget, have no choice but to send her to the less expensive state school. Even though she's less than thrilled about it, I'm sure she will take the place by storm. She's a good girl although she made a poor choice, but she seems to have risen above her trials.

Not everyone has our kind of emotional support from family and friends, so we are all lucky that way. But then, not everyone has children who are prodigies like Maggie and I do. It's nice that they've found their niches so early in their lives. I certainly struggled with it all when I was coming along. I had the talent, the gift of playing by ear that Myers has inherited from me, but not the nerves, and as a result, not the necessary courage to display my gift to the world. At least being the village's dermatologist has allowed me to help people. I know every third person here, since they have all walked into my office for treatment of one ailment or another, acne breakouts, Botox injections, and the constant skin cancer surveillances I do.

"I'm sorry you won't let us take care of Howard while you're away. He'd be good company," I say, stroking the golden's silky ear, making him gaze soulfully at me and pant with pleasure.

"Well, I knew you were going out of town to get Myers settled into his program, and besides, it'll be nice for you to be a bit footloose and fancy free for a little while. Howard loves the kennel and will have lots of attention. It's like going to camp for him!" he laughs.

"Okay, well, I hope you and Mom have a great trip. Don't get sick, and take lots of pictures."

Before he can say, "You know I will," we hear the motor from my ex-husband Kent's SUV purr around the corner and stop. I sigh silently, wishing he would have just idled in front of the house and let Myers off, as he usually would. There's no reason to stop, but I guess seeing Dad's car, Kent might feel this is a good opportunity to put on a show for him. He has always tried to kiss up to my father, despite *all* we know about him. Some things never change. Dad's deadpan expression tells me he is thinking the same thing. We truly are on the same wavelength this morning!

Kent is the last person I want to see today. I don't want him here, interfering with my remembrances of Stan. Regardless of what else is going on, it is still Stan's day. As Dad and I pop our heads out the front door, we hear the trunk open and close as Myers retrieves his backpack from Kent's SUV, and next comes Kent's greeting.

"Hello, Dandy! Didn't expect to see you here!" he exclaims, bounding up the steps in cargo shorts and a T-shirt to shake hands with my father, as if they are old friends. He is slapping my dad on the shoulder and Dad is reciprocating coolly, keeping up the facade, if only for Myers's sake.

"Good morning, Kent. Nice to see you, too! Hi, Myers! How was the camping trip? You must have left at the crack of dawn."

"It was a great trip!" Kent nods his head in my direction and says wryly, as if, of course, it is my fault and he has had to make yet another sacrifice on my behalf, "Susannah wanted me to get Myers back early since they've got to be over in Winston after lunchtime."

"Hey! Dandy! You brought Howard!" says Myers, breaking into a grin. He sinks immediately to a squat and takes Howard's head in his hands, fondling his ears, giving him a proper hello. "Hey, Buddy!"

Ah, yes, it is my fault. Whatever it is, it is always my fault. If Kent Morgan had had the situation his way, they'd still be camping on Crowder Mountain, but I'm sure Myers was glad to break camp and leave as early as possible. Saying things are strained between the two of them is being generous. Myers comes through the front door, laden with his backpack, giving me a hug, seeming even taller and manlier than when he left yesterday. His longish brown hair is unruly as I expected, and he smells like a mixture of campfire, musty clothes, and that out-of-doors smell that a shower will erase in no time. I sniff one more time, satisfied to pick out the scent of sunscreen that Myers has had the good sense to use, no doubt only because he knows there will be hell to pay from me if he doesn't wear it. At least I have won that battle.

"Hey, Mom," he greets me, his voice characteristically hoarse and soft.

"Hi, hon. How was it?" I ask, innocently, accepting his quick kiss on my cheek. He glances at the robe for an instant and sends me a knowing look. There is a frisson of sympathy and understanding in his round brown eyes, so like mine, and I love him even more for that.

"It was great. Dad killed a copperhead," he says without emotion, moving past me toward the kitchen. My son runs deep; I'm sure this information is just the tip of the iceberg. We, too, maintain the show for civility's sake.

"Oh. Wow! I'm glad you both made it back in one piece."

Kent stands, hands on hips, appraising me. "Nice robe."

"Thanks; it's my favorite." I give him polite eye contact but nothing more. He has no idea about today's significance, and I have no intention of mentioning it to him.

"Are you hungry, kiddo?" I ask Myers, glad to change the subject.

"Nope, we stopped for chicken biscuits on the way home. I'm good. What I really need is a shower."

He is trying to ditch his father, which I can totally understand. They were supposed to have a big talk last night. It was *The Big Talk* that Kent had promised Myers when he turned eighteen, when Kent thought he'd be old enough to understand what had transpired between the two of us. Personally, I thought it seemed a little late to be explaining things because over the past eleven years, I have been grappling with the delicate balance of answering Myers's questions discreetly out of respect for Kent's privacy, regardless of how disgusted I have been with his errant behavior the whole time. I'm not an angel, but compared to Kent Morgan, I'm at least singing in the church choir balcony in the eyes of anyone who knows us, and knows all that's gone on since I've known him. Even Myers has professed to me on occasion, and probably to his closest friends, that he thinks his father is a jerk. For me, though, in the presence of our son, restraint is hard. I can't tell Myers that I concur because he and his father should be allowed to have their own relationship without my influence, in hopes that someday Myers will learn to trust and love Kent. I know

Myers is fully capable of making up his own mind. The magical age of adulthood makes understanding our situation no easier. Still, I have to say I'm delighted that Myers seems to have the proper insight to know I have always had his best interests at heart. My son has shown me nothing but love and respect. How could he not?

I reach up to ruffle his hair, and he gives me a brave smile. He knows it's Stan Day, and I see his eyes move to the kitchen counter where there is a package of cinnamon rolls waiting to be baked in the oven—Stan's favorite decadent breakfast. I'm glad I waited to pop them in the oven so I wouldn't have to explain it all to Kent.

"Oh, and look what Dandy and Mima have brought you for your concerts!" I tell Myers, lifting up the black shirt for his inspection.

"Wow! Sweet!" he says, grinning and examining the shirt while I hold up the cuff so he can see the cufflinks. "Thanks, Dandy!"

Kent is making conversation with my father, asking all about the trip to China. Dad is giving him the brief synopsis, subtly mentioning that he is on the way to drop off Howard at the kennel before he and my mother are due at the airport. Kent nods vigorously, knowing that my sister is providing their ride. She and my parents live in Magnolia Village as well. After Mom and Dad retired here years ago, Stan and I followed. Then came Jen, to pursue the excellent real estate opportunities the community offered. Although all three of our families live separately, for most people, it might be too close for comfort, having all that family around, but we are comfortable with it. At least, we *were* comfortable with it until Kent just about made the situation unbearable. He continues to live in Charlotte, in a swanky high-rise condo in Uptown, but it seems he is in Magnolia Village all the time. It all makes for such awkward small-town kinds of moments, but I try to deal with it the best I can for Myers's sake. Now, to get Kent on his merry way....

"Thanks so much for dropping Myers off on time. I'm glad neither of you was snake-bit!"

Kent eyes me, as if he really doesn't believe me, as though I'd really wished the opposite, but I am truly thankful that Myers is safe, and glad not to be dealing with an emergency involving my ex-husband. He takes the hint as Dad hugs me and tells Howard it's time to go.

"Thanks for the shirt, Dandy. Tell Meems thanks, too. Have a great trip!" says Myers.

He and my father give each other the customary, manly hugs and backslaps, and then my father kisses him European-style on the cheek.

"I'll tell her, Myers. Have a *wonderful* chamber music experience. You'll love the School of the Arts! Give my best to Maggie and Casey!"

With one more meaningful hug for me, my father is off with Howard padding softly behind him. Kent follows them awkwardly through the living room, bidding us goodbye as well. There is no hug for him from our son, but an "Enjoyed it, Dad," over his shoulder as Myers slings the backpack over his shoulder and heads for the laundry room.

"Bye, Kent. Thanks again for getting him home on time," I add at his retreating back, as if he is a neighbor who has dropped off my newspaper. It is so easy to dismiss this man and get back to the important men in my life. I have made it a habit to block out all my memories of him—as soon as they happen! Back in my kitchen, I go to the cupboard for the baking stone, and I knock the tube of cinnamon rolls on the counter to open them. Thankful, although a bit awestruck that he is depositing his dirty clothes without being told, I can hear Myers bumping around in the laundry room, and then he appears again. I am so happy to see him. Since graduation, he has hardly been around, away on lake trips with friends and occupied with music commitments. For me, his entire senior year has been a gradual foray into being alone, which I believe I've managed decently, but the real test will be when he leaves for college in a few short weeks.

"Do I have time for a quick shower?"

"Sure. The timing will be just right," I say, peeling the wrapper off the rolls. Myers is at my elbow, watching for a minute before I feel another quick kiss on the side of my head. I feel a little tingle at this rare display of my almost-grown son's affection that makes me want to freeze time. Guarding my delighted and surprised reaction, I hold my breath, hoping not to spoil my chances of it reoccurring at some later time. Still, I glance up at him to show my appreciation.

"I miss him too, Mom." His long, lovely fingers stroke the robe's flannel sleeve, and with that, he is tromping upstairs to take his shower. However, before the shower water begins, I hear him on the violin. Thinking I'll change out of Stan's robe while the pastries bake, I separate the rolls from the tube, arranging them on the stone, listening to Myers's warm-up. After a few runs to wake up his fingers, he begins to crank out a spirited rendition of "The Devil Went Down to Georgia."

I laugh to myself, hearing Stan's laughter as well, booming inside my head. After the soccer accident that left his vocal cords slightly altered, he has tended to express himself in alternative ways—music being his preference. My son has an excellent sense of humor, which was appreciated by Stan even more than by Kent. It's why Myers was always closer to Stan; that, and so many other reasons. Stan had that initial connection, a unique calming ability manifested in his bedside manner, with everyone. He conveyed total trust, an important quality that made him the revered doctor he was, but even more than that, he had the ability to listen, making whomever he was talking to feel important and valued, something Myers needed from someone besides me in the first days of my separation from Kent. Stan was a man of his word, and he lived an honorable and abundant life, making our lives fuller for our association with him. Myers didn't need me to tell him that; he knew it for himself from the day they met when Stan cared for him in the hospital's emergency room. And as weird as things got for one reason or another, Myers's opinion of Kent deteriorated rapidly, ratcheting down one event at a time, until I feared for that conversation they apparently had last night around their campfire. Although Myers seems unaffected by their time together, I'm sure his silence for now is just his typical way of dealing with life, and that there is more to what he's feeling than he's willing to show. I hope Myers will share the details of that conversation with me at some point. I would love to hear Kent's explanation of what went wrong with us, of what he did, of why he left us....

Of why he feels the need to date my *sister.*

Chapter 2

MYERS

In the time it has taken our decadent cinnamon rolls to bake, I have started Myers's laundry and changed from Stan's robe into a loose summer dress, a cheerful burgundy and rose-pink print, perfect for the day's activities, and dinner later on this evening. I have lifted the buns from the baking stone onto our plates, and I am pouring orange juice when Myers reenters the kitchen, dressed in shorts, deck shoes, and a T-shirt, advertising one of his favorite bands, with his wet, dark hair fingered in place. He smells clean and I keep forgetting how tall he's growing, as he towers over me, while following me to the table and carrying the orange juice glasses. His acne is clearing up, I notice with satisfaction as he sits around the corner from me in our usual places. There is so much I want to know about his time with Kent that the questions scream inside me, although I forcibly feign my placid expression and restrain myself for his benefit, and perhaps my own.

Did he drink? What did he say about Jen? Did he tell you why he didn't show up at the hospital when you got kicked in the throat during your soccer game ten years ago? Did he tell you why he left us?

I can't ask any of these questions, yet, at least. Myers takes a large bite from one of his cinnamon rolls, eliminating half of it as I watch. He seems so calm. He has been so adept over the years at hiding his feelings, so it is hard for even me to tell what's going on in that head of his. He should appear slightly nervous since he's getting ready to depart for yet another musical study program, complete with all the post-high school drama that will no doubt accompany the experience, yet he feasts on breakfast as if our next stop will be the mailbox, or the grocery store, or walking next door to feed Mrs. Miller's cat.

He catches me watching him, throwing me off kilter by his unexpected comment. "You look pretty, Mom. New dress?"

"Oh, thanks, honey. Yeah, I went shopping after work yesterday. I thought it would be nice to have something new and cool for the summer. Something casual for when I'm not at the office."

He nods thoughtfully, studying me as he chews his roll. My new dress will most likely be my summer uniform away from work. Normally, I don't enjoy shopping, but I will have to find something to do with my time when Myers is gone. He has been in and out all summer, entertaining his new freedom, but I know that when he leaves for college in August, I will feel utterly alone, something I'm not anticipating with a joyful heart. *It's all right*, Stan says to me.

Still Myers is looking at me with a new interest. His hair is beginning to dry around the ends, and it lifts away from his round face in attractive waves. His earnest brown eyes study me, making me aware of the effect he will have on the new girls he meets. I feel a catch in my heart. There will be so many new possibilities for my Myers, starting possibly today. There has not been a special girl for him, except for Hannah McIntyre, a girl from one of the music camps last summer. He'd taken a liking to her and finally gotten up the nerve to declare it, just when she'd chosen another boy in the program, cutting my son to shreds in the process. He's played his affections closer to his chest since then. Aside from his best friend, Casey French, Myers has had little female companionship lately with anyone his age. Because of Myers's reflective, pensive nature, laced with his refreshingly dry wit, Casey exasperates him at times with her manic sense of humor and moodiness, but he tolerates her loyally for her obvious devotion to him. They have been tied together like kindred spirits by their music since the day Myers picked up my violin and Casey her cello. If there is any one of his peers he respects, it is Casey.

Licking the icing off his fingers, Myers says thoughtfully, "Do you still have any of Stan's ties?"

Feeling as though I've been caught red-handed in my private stash of Stan's clothes, I inhale unexpectedly. "Yes. They're in his closet. Do you want some of them?"

"Maybe. I was hoping there'd be one to go with my new shirt."

"Look through them and take whatever you want. How are you coming on your packing?"

"Five minutes I'll be done."

I can stand it no longer. "So, how was the camping trip?"

Myers regards me warily as if I really don't want to hear about it. If I wait, he will tell me. Maybe.

He takes a deep breath and exhales slowly, wiping his fingers on his napkin and casting his eyes around the room. "Well, there was no beer, if that's what you're wondering."

I shake my head (but I really *was* wondering) and give him an indulgent look.

He shrugs. "Dad is always telling me that I should be able to drink a beer if I'm old enough to go and serve my country. You know, I can get shot at, or blown to bits by an IED, but I can't drink a stinking beer. But, you'll be glad to know, he did not bring beer on the trip, like the good Boy Scout leader he is...was."

It's true. Kent was Myers's Boy Scout leader for a time. None of the boys liked him particularly because he was so harsh with them, and just a little too cocky for the tastes of all the parents involved, so after a couple of the boys dropped out of the troop, and a few painful discussions with two of the other dads, Kent stepped aside, and another leader was assigned. Kent is probably still sore about it, and of course, holds it against me, thinking I started it all, but I had nothing to do with it. Over the years, Kent had made sure that Myers got all the hiking, boating, and camping experiences he thought a boy should have, and despite whatever differences they have, Myers has loved it all. It was a good way for them to spend time together on their every-other-weekend visits. They were able to build their bond without my being in the picture, and admittedly, I am grateful for that.

"Did you have your big powwow then?"

"Yep." Myers takes his time drinking his juice. "You really don't want to hear about it, do you, Mom?"

"I don't know. But I am curious. He always said he'd explain everything when you turned eighteen. So I can't help but wonder what in the world he could tell you now that you haven't already figured out on your own."

Myers is quiet a moment and then looks at me. "It was just a lot of words...you know?" After another moment of staring darkly at the table, he begins. "He told me he had an affair with Penny. I didn't know *that*. It happened during the time when I got kicked in the throat. He was with her when you took me to the hospital and you couldn't get in touch with him—the day we met Stan for the first time."

I nod. So far, Kent has told the truth. Myers never knew about the affair with Penny, Kent's saucy little paralegal. Smarter than I'd given her credit for being, she'd had the sense to move on eventually, but I suppose, as Myers grew older, he suspected something of the sort had happened. Myers knew Penny, and that the affair happened in Kent's law offices with her was probably quite a shock for him. It certainly was for me. Now I watch as the resulting anger is registering on his face, requiring a few moments for him to compose himself before proceeding with the rest of it.

"And then he talked about how he used to drink too much and how sorry he is about it all. He talked about that night when he got angry with you and threw a beer bottle at you—when we came to spend the night with Dandy and Mima. I remember him throwing that bottle at you, thinking he had to be kidding around. I remember that like it was yesterday. When I realized it wasn't a joke, I was so scared, like—sick to my stomach that Dad would do that to you. When you're little and you see something like that, you don't know how to react, you know? I didn't understand what was happening. I just thought it was awful, and that I wanted to get out of there. I knew it was bad when you told me we were going to Dandy and Mima's to spend the night. And then on the way we had that wreck and ended up back in the ER with Stan—again."

I swallow just thinking about it. For Myers, it must have been terrifying. Finding Stan again in the ER that night must have been nothing short of divine intervention. I was so relieved to find a friendly face, but I'd had no idea how much would change for all of us that night. From that night on, Stan had been forever in our picture. He had been concerned about us initially the day I'd brought Myers to the emergency room. Myers had been kicked in the throat during a soccer game when he was eight years old, and I'd brought him to the hospital's ER to have him checked over for any tracheal damage. After the initial triage and Stan's expert assessment of Myers's airway, bleeding, and circulation, I was impressed that he'd ordered an otolaryngology consultation to ensure Myers had no further damage that might have escaped Stan's examination. During the ear, nose, and throat doctor's visit with Myers, I couldn't escape Stan's steady, inquisitive gaze, assessing me, too, as if I were his patient as well, the way he'd focused on me each time I'd tried to reach Kent on the phone. I had just shrugged and said, "He must be in a meeting." Then Stan had asked quietly and respectfully, "On a Saturday?" A month later, after the beer bottle incident, we'd reappeared in the ER, making Stan's radar go off again about what was happening with us. About what was happening with *me*. I was so distracted on the drive to my parents' house that night that I ran a stop sign and got T-boned on the driver's side of the car, but mercifully, I escaped with only a couple of broken ribs, soreness, and bruising. Although Myers was unhurt physically, he was considerably shaken up emotionally. It occurred to me in the hospital that Stan was more attentive toward me than necessary, although I liked it. I liked *him*. I particularly liked the way he paid attention to Myers while I was being looked after. Stan called me several times after that and never left us feeling alone.

The memories make me sigh. "It does seem like yesterday. All of it does. I tried to protect you, but I couldn't. You were only eight years old. No child needs to go through any of that kind of emotional trauma. You knew far too much."

Myers presses his lips together. The same red lips I have. Looking at him is like looking in a mirror sometimes, seeing a masculine version of myself.

"I knew a lot. So, back to our conversation last night…. After all of that, Dad didn't tell me anything else I didn't know. Except that he kept apologizing for the way it all fell apart, that it was never *my* fault, and that if he could make it up to me, he would. Like he could possibly erase any of that now by just saying he's sorry. I never thought it was *my* fault. Why would he think that? Does he think kids are *stupid?* Did he think I was that stupid?"

I shrug. "No. You are certainly not stupid. And you never were." Regretfully, my son is more like a friend to commiserate with than a child I should be raising. His conversation with Kent must have been painful.

"I'm sorry."

"Don't be, Mom. You can just—stop being sorry. None of this has ever been your fault. I've always known that. And I guess I accept *his* apology, but it just seems sort of meaningless now. It all just sounded like a bunch of words today…. I don't know."

Too little, too late. I sigh again, relieved in a way that he realizes I wasn't to blame. At least I had found the courage to get us out when I did. Stan helped me find that courage. "And Jen? What did he tell you about Jen?" I shake curls back from my face and watch his expression shift from anger to discomfort.

"We didn't talk about her much," he says, looking down at the napkin in his hand. "If anybody's stupid, it's her. Sorry; I mean, she's your sister and all, but—you know. Why does she keep dating him? And he shouldn't go out with her because of you. They're both ridiculous. It's disgusting. That's why Sloan never comes home anymore. And Trip is the same way. I think Jen believes Dad wants to marry her, but he told me he won't ever get married again, that he's really not good at being married."

It's my turn to press my lips together. As much as my sister has sabotaged her own family, I know she won't want to hear this news. I wonder whether Kent has shared his opinions on marriage with her. It's a shame that she has perpetuated their relationship, to the point where she has alienated her grown children. As much as she pretends for my sake that her relationship with Kent is casual, I think she's been banking on someday having his income to fill in her financial gaps since she and her husband split up years ago when she came to Magnolia to try her hand at real estate in the village. Like any single parent would, when Sloan and Trip were in college, she struggled with money. More recently, her real estate commissions have suffered due to the economic downturn, even in Magnolia. Aside from the awkwardness of the situation, there is also the issue of Kent's past infidelity with me. I warned her: *Once a cheater, always a cheater,* but has she listened to me? I hate to see her get hurt, but I'm afraid she will at some point. Oh, there is so much divorce and dysfunction among us! We are a disappointing lot, to say the least. It seems that most of Myers's friends come from broken homes, except for his best friends, Tim and Casey. I hate to think of ours as a broken home, but divorce has left us unmistakably broken in its ugly wake, and my son has borne the brunt of all of our failed relationships. When Stan came into the picture, our wounds started to heal, but then he was ripped mercilessly from us in an instant.

What can I tell Myers to make him feel better? Being a single mother has forced me to play my hand without reservation many times. It's important for me to tell him the truths I've gleaned, and I have yet another teachable moment at hand.

"Well, honey, I'm sure you've taken plenty of notes from what you've seen in your short life. I don't want you to dwell on the negative feelings you might have about your dad, but the one thing you can take away from all of this is how *not* to behave when you find the girl who's right for you. Or anyone you love, for that matter. You're steadfast, and I love that about you. You know how to be generous and trustworthy and how to be someone's true friend. You know?"

"I know, Mom," he says quietly after a moment, giving me a little shrug, but I make him look at me.

"That's really special, Myers. With all you've been through, it's amazing that you can give of yourself the way you do. And when you think you're ready to get married—one day—*far* into the future!" I laugh, "Remember this; marriage isn't about *you*. It's about the one you love. It's about making that person happy. Make sure you find someone who feels the same way. Your dad and I obviously didn't learn that important lesson. But Stan taught me that, and you should take it to heart. I was blessed with a second chance, you know? We both were."

"You were happy."

I nod, giving him a little smile at his understatement. The love, trust, and security we both felt from Stan were boundless, making it so easy to give it all back to him. And to think it all started with one—or two innocent hospital visits. Even my parents were swept in by his charisma the night they came to pick us up. Stan left such an impression on all of us that Mima even took a photograph of him and Myers together when she and Dad rescued us at the hospital.

"He always treated you with respect. And he treated me that way, too. That's the kind of man I want to be. It just really sucks that he's gone."

"Yes. I know. It really does suck." I wait just a moment and let the thoughts sink in, warmed and grateful that Myers loved Stan so much, that he isn't railing against Kent, and that he can appreciate the blessings we've had in our lives. Perhaps the anger he used to hold inside is waning. He seems to have sorted himself all out. It's what I've always prayed for. My son is suddenly very grown up!

Stacking our plates to carry away from the table, I start to stand up, and then Myers says, "Do you think you'll find another guy? I mean, it's been three years...." He searches my face and I wonder whether he knows he's knocked the wind out of me. The empathy in his eyes makes tears prick the backs of my eyelids. But it's a fair question so I stop and look him squarely in the eye.

"To tell you the truth, I really haven't wanted to find someone else."

"Well, when I go away to Belmont, I don't want you to be lonely."

It's a sweet thought, coming from my boy. *Lonely*.... Myers isn't just talking about getting a dog; although, we have talked about getting another dog for company. When Hank, our rescue dog from the animal shelter, died, it was too painful even thinking about replacing him. Between Myers's music and our lust for new places and adventures, we traveled so much that it didn't make sense being tied down to a pet, so we'd let the idea go. Introvert that I am, I enjoy being by myself, but being *lonely* haunts me. I *have* thought about being lonely a lot, especially today. But another man? I really don't want another man. No one else I could ever meet would be able to top Stan. I'm forty-eight years old, although people tell me I look like thirty-something, so maybe I could even be somewhat marketable. At times, I do miss physical contact and find myself wondering whether I'll ever have sex again. Still, I don't think I need anyone else in my life. Even for company.

I'd rather not have Myers see my inner struggle so I answer as resolutely as possible. "Nonsense. How can I be lonely with Maggie and Barb and my other friends to keep me company? Besides, I'm too busy to be lonely. You know...I run most mornings, and a couple of times a week, I go to Pilates with Maggie. In the evenings, I read, or play the piano, or watch movies when I'm here. I was thinking about joining a book club and taking a photography class. I even thought about starting a dinner group. Maybe I'll learn to sail or something. See, since I'm going to be an empty-nester, I've been making a list of things to do so there's no way I'll be lonely. So don't worry about me, okay? I will miss *you*, though!" I smile so he'll be reassured. The last thing I want is his worrying about me.

He looks at me and blinks. "Okay. Wow. You have been thinking about it."

"Okay, then. So let's finish getting you packed. Maggie and Casey will be here in half an hour."

"No, they won't. They're always late," he says, stretching his arms over his head, tossing his napkin onto his plate and yawning largely.

"Then come and check out Stan's ties," I say as he helps me carry the dishes to the dishwasher. After that job is finished, I move his washed clothes into the dryer, thinking he won't need these clothes for his couple of weeks away at NCSA, but still, they need to be dried before we leave town. On my way upstairs, I check the air conditioning, turning it up to 78 degrees until I return tomorrow.

Later in my bedroom, I assemble toiletries for my overnight bag while Myers looks through Stan's closet for a suitable tie. Suddenly, he turns to me with questioning eyes.

"Uh...Mom, how long are you going to keep Stan's clothes around?"

I swallow, realizing I have been caught doing something unacceptable. It occurs to me that Myers hasn't laid eyes inside Stan's closet since he died. I realize also that my reluctance to part with his clothing has appeared rather ghastly to my son. His eyes hold me to the task I've avoided for so long. I did away with most of Stan's other things, except his guitar and a mandolin that Myers wanted, some tools, his water skis, and his fishing tackle. Maybe it really is time I should do something about his clothes. It's been three years, after all. *But I will keep the robe.*

"Well," I clear my throat, "I don't know. I guess I should take care of it while you're gone. Actually, I was waiting until you grew into his clothes to see if there's anything you'd want. Do you see a tie you like?"

"Yeah," he says quietly, slipping a couple over his hand, one with a black and silver pattern that will go nicely with his new shirt.

"Do you want to try on any of his jackets?"

He looks through the closet again, fingering the leather jacket and the other sport coats.

"No.... But I definitely want his leather jacket. Save that, okay?" he says and watches me a minute before going back to his room.

I feel rattled, but I proceed routinely with my packing, placing the gift from my parents into the bag, folding a pair of jeans, a blouse, a couple of pairs of underwear, and my favorite pajamas, packing them with my shower kit into my bag. It's when I zip it shut that Stan speaks to me again. *It's time to let go.* His voice sounds so real that there is no mistaking it is truly audible.

"What?" I murmur, looking around.

Myers sticks his head in my door. "I said, 'It's time to go.' Maggie's in the driveway. Didn't you hear her honk the horn? She's *early* for a change!"

Chapter 3

....

THE FRENCH GIRLS

....

Maggie French owns the biggest SUV I have ever seen. I know little about cars, apart from my Prius, which gets unbelievable gas mileage, but with Casey's cello and both our children's luggage, whatever it is that Maggie drives is the vehicle that can hold it all. Myers is irritated that he can't just drive himself in his own car, but the camp doesn't allow its students to have their cars on campus. That's one problem none of us has to worry about! He is much too independent for his own good at times.

"Heeeyyy!" Maggie shouts, climbing down from her rig to give me a hug. Her short figure looks funny disembarking from such a large vehicle. I can hear Casey's infectious giggle as Myers saunters over to her side of the car to give her a hug. Maggie is forever in a good mood, which is a helpful attribute on a day like today, and I'm sure she knows it. She's one of those friends *who knows the song in your heart, and can sing it back to you when you forget the words.* That was said of Stan at his memorial service, and I love it. It was Stan all over, and it is also my friend Maggie.

"Hey, you!" I give her an extra squeeze and a smile to reassure her I am okay, making her wink at me. Brushing her thick chestnut hair away from her china doll's face, she grins back, her bright blue eyes sparkling as usual. She has mastered the use of a flat iron. On other days, her hair would be as full of curls as mine, but not today. As always, she looks perfect. Her makeup is impeccable, though subtle, making me wonder whether my mineral powder and light lip gloss have brightened me up this morning. I am forever trying to tone down my red lips. With my pale skin, big dark eyes and almost black hair, I can look like a horror film character if I don't soften my Gothic looks. Thank God my mother taught me early on how to style myself during those boney, gawky, middle school years, encouraging me to stand up straight, showing me how to tame my wild curls, giving me makeup lessons, and teaching me to pluck my eyebrows so I didn't look like the Bride of Frankenstein. If I look wretched now, Maggie doesn't react, so maybe my 3 a.m. morning hasn't affected me the way I thought.

It's only been since Wednesday that we went to our Pilates class together, but we always greet each other with enthusiasm. Casey and Myers, on the other hand, have been apart since graduation so they'll have a lot of catching up to do. They are Mutt and Jeff as always. Casey is short and plump in stark contrast to Myers's tall lanky frame, and he is lifting her off the ground comically in one of his great bear hugs, sending her into a fit of giggles. Her laugh is like no other—a combination of a machine gun and the little chipmunks I remember from the old Alvin cartoons. Casey shares her mother's exuberance, while Myers is consummately laidback, but as talented as these two children are, there is no wonder they have a strong bond. Casey chatters away and I wonder how long it will take before Myers is able to get in a word, while Maggie raises the tailgate, taking charge of loading the SUV.

"Okay! Thank goodness boys travel light! Casey has enough stuff to outfit every girl at camp! Here, hon, let me have Myers's hang-ups and I'll put 'em right here," she says, reaching inside the back door and hanging his dress shirts with Casey's assorted black dresses. "Look at this nice black shirt!"

"Oh, that doesn't look like much," I say, noticing Casey's one large suitcase, patterned with black and white flowers, reminiscent of the '60s, and two additional smaller bags. "I was expecting steamer trunks and hat boxes!"

Casey shrieks with laughter. "She made me leave my boas and hats at home, Susannah!" she says, coming around to the back of the car to hug me.

"How *are* you, sweet girl? And how was your drama camp experience? I heard you were a smash in *Hairspray!*"

"It was such a blast! And it was so much nicer having the lead from the start! Not like being the understudy who cashed in on someone else's bad luck, you know?"

I nod, understanding her reference to the part she played in their high school production of *South Pacific* in the spring, when the girl who had been cast as Nellie Forbush had come down with a stomach virus and Casey had filled in at the last minute, playing the part brilliantly. Casey didn't get the part originally because of her weight, but when she took the stage, no one noticed how much she weighed, and the overall effect of her acting was simply dazzling. And who knew the girl could sing and dance? This little girl who'd spent her childhood immersed in the piano and the cello was truly a star in every way.

"Well, I'm sure you were great, and I'm sorry I missed it! Myers has missed *you* terribly!"

He grins, shoving his small bag and violin case into the back of the car, and closes the tailgate, giving Maggie the hug she's been waiting for. "Hey, Maggie!"

"Myers! Oh my gosh, you've grown a foot!" She shoots her sapphire eyes my way. "What have you been feeding him, Susannah? Plant food?"

"Oh, that's what the blue Kool-Aid was, Mom?" he jokes back, making Maggie laugh.

"As if you have ever tasted Kool-Aid!" I chortle, seating myself in the passenger seat.

"Oh, how about *Spam?* I ate Spam for the first time at drama camp!" Casey giggles again, climbing into the backseat and slamming her door.

"Gross! *Why?*"asks Myers.

"Just to say I'd done it. Have you ever had Twinkies?"

"Where did you get your hands on a Twinkie?" asks Maggie, since we are all aware that the calorie-laden little snack was taken off the market last fall.

"My roommate had them. Her mother hoarded a bunch of boxes of Twinkies when the bankruptcy announcement came out. But now you can buy them in the stores again. Did you know that? Have you ever sucked the cream out of one?" she is shrieking again at Myers's disgusted facial expression.

"You've really walked on the wild side since I've last seen you," he tells her as she continues to giggle from the backseat while Maggie and I exchange skeptical looks. "I'll be watching you for the next couple of weeks."

"Please do! Keep her out of trouble, Myers!" Maggie pleads to him in the rearview mirror, as she drives us out of Magnolia Village toward the interstate.

"It's a dirty job, but somebody has to do it, I guess," he says, his hoarse voice just over a whisper, the residual effect of his soccer injury, despite speech therapy. The sound of it is endearing to me, and everyone else too, I suppose. There is nothing like loving your own child, and I feel a small burst of pride that he is a good friend as well as being my baby. My very tall and manly prodigy baby.

The four of us talk nonstop for the next hour and a half up Interstate 85 until we reach Winston-Salem and Maggie suggests lunch at Sweet Potatoes restaurant. Maggie and I have been dying to eat there. After a couple of unsuccessful passes down the busy street in search of a parking place, she parks in the parking deck and we walk down Trade Street until we see the sign that lets us know we are in the right place.

"Oh my God, is that your stomach growling?" Casey asks Myers as we pour over the menu.

"Yeah, probably. I'm starving!"

"What else is new?" I ask, knowing it's true. Myers has eaten me out of house and home since he was ten years old.

There is far too much decadent and delicious food on this menu. Our server appears to take our order. Maggie and I order water with lemon, Myers, a half-and-half tea, and Casey orders a Pepsi with two cherries.

At the table next to us, a blonde with bee-stung lips is chatting on her cell phone while her irritated male companion looks on, tapping his fingers on the table.

Casey plays at pressing and stretching out her lips, attempting to look like the blonde, to no avail, sending her and Myers laughing again. She launches into a new character at once.

"Hi, I'm *Chardonnay.*" She tries for sultry, like the blonde who is completely oblivious to Casey's shenanigans.

"Sounds like a stripper," Myers says, his head in his menu.

She giggles, continuing. "Chardonnay French. It's my stage name. I really like it when I have to write my last name first. Then I'm *French Chardonnay!*" she says, giving Myers an impressive pout, then spilling into her chipmunk giggles again, attracting the attention of other diners next to us, and drawing a snort and a head shake from Myers. Maggie and I laugh too, but try to ignore her, turning our full attention to the menu. Lively jazz playing in the background has each of us tapping a different body part as we pour over our menus. The food options make for difficult decisions. Maggie chooses the Portobello mushroom sandwich with goat cheese on a sweet potato bun, while I opt for the curried chicken salad. We are planning to eat dinner later at the Salem Tavern in Old Salem, and I don't relish being full from lunch when the time arrives. It's best to pace oneself. As I predict, Myers and Casey order the "Hamsome," a ham and melted cheese sandwich on a sweet potato roll with sweet potato fries on the side. Watching the plates coming out of the kitchen and smelling the delicious aromas, we promise ourselves another trip to this place, and we haven't even tasted the food yet!

The conversation finally turns to the upcoming chamber music camp and Casey needles Myers just like I'd expected. She folds her hands across the table and smiles. Her lank, dishwater blond hair, having escaped its ponytail, hangs in mussed waves around her face, which is devoid of makeup, but her sparkling eyes and matching grin make her characteristically disarming.

"Is Hannah McIntyre coming this year?"

Myers groans. "Don't know. Don't care."

"Right! She'll probably be in your quartet at one time or another."

Myers gives a noncommittal shrug and says nothing.

"Why isn't Mrs. Linden teaching here this summer?" he asks us, obviously attempting a topic change. Barbara Linden has been their violin and cello teacher for as many years as I can remember, and she has often offered her teaching services at the nearby chamber music programs during the summers.

Maggie looks to me for answers. "I don't remember why not; do you, Susannah?"

"She and Richard are going to visit their daughter and grandchildren. Her daughter has a new baby. She did say they'd be back in time for your final concert."

"I miss her!" says Casey. "It's going to be fun having other teachers, but not everyone is as funny as Barb." Casey is the only student who gets away with calling our friend Barb. And Barb has that kind of dry wit we all appreciate, even though she is a formidable and demanding teacher who expects nothing but perfection, but these two can handle it. Nothing rattles or flusters Casey French.

Our food arrives and we tuck in gratefully. I was hungry after all. We eat in silence except for a few "Mmmms" and "Ohhhs!" as the food exceeds our expectations. I watch our two children eating, thinking it's odd how their personas change dramatically when they take the stage during their performances. Casey's piano performance of George Gershwin's "Rhapsody in Blue" comes to mind incongruently somehow, as I watch her take a hefty bite of her yummy looking ham sandwich.

What a different picture she was that evening back in March when she walked onto the stage and took her place at the grand piano in front of the high school symphony. The band and orchestra had joined forces to produce a stunning rendition of one of my favorite musical pieces ever, and I was thrilled for Casey to have the spotlight. I remember shivering as she seemed to glide across the stage to the audience's polite applause. Her shoulders were thrown back with a show of confident energy. Her hair was styled in Marcel waves around her face, shining like honey under the lights, and she wore an elegant sheath of a gown, with a sheer overlay that floated down with long fringe past her elbows—ice blue, shot with silver threads that picked up the spotlight, making us gasp and murmur. If there were ever a vision of Roaring Twenties opulence, it was Casey French that night! When she seated herself on the piano bench and waited through the clarinet overture, and then began the dramatic piece, we were all star-struck. Her fingers danced effortlessly over the keys as she played without the music. I can still remember the goose bumps that rose on my arms during that heady and fearless music, so exciting and reminiscent of the 1920s. I'm sure many Casey French fans were born that night. Not to mention George Gershwin fans as well.

And here is this young woman who unabashedly sucks the cream out of Hostess Twinkies and teases my son relentlessly about his woebegone love life, wiping bread crumbs off her face, and drinking Pepsi—with two cherries. She lives her life to the absolute fullest, reminding me to take good notes while we are all together today.

"What's making you smile, Susannah?" she asks, those eyes of hers filled with mischief.

"I can't help thinking about your 'Rhapsody in Blue' performance last spring."

"God! What made you think of that?" she asks, laughing, and shooting a glance at Myers.

"I don't know. I always get these images of you both in one performance or another when you're doing the most mundane things, like eating, for example."

Myers grins and pops another sweet potato fry into his mouth. "You're so weird, Mom."

"I know. And so are you, so I guess it runs in the family."

"Isn't it fun that we all have such vivid imaginations?" asks Maggie, and we all agree with her.

"That's why it's so much fun being together," I say, nodding. We are usually doubled over with laughter after people-watching, hamming it up for Maggie's camera, or taking a situation and putting a ridiculous spin on it, or just being happy, listening to some new music or an old treasure. There is never a dull moment with the four of us, and it doesn't take television or video games to amuse us. All of that seems like anesthesia for unfulfilled living, and I was grateful that Stan saw it all the same way as well.

"So much fun, so little time!" says Casey, dissolving into giggles. "Oh, Susannah!" she says and then she laughs again at herself, as my name has forever been the butt of jokes, making me shake my head. "Susannah Myers. I love your name." She looks like she might do something with it, like she did with Chardonnay French.

"Susannah Brody," I correct her, not willing to give up Stan, but I, too, have always loved the sound of my maiden name, which is obviously why I named my only son Myers. It suits him: tall, sensitive and serious, with his witty streak appearing at the most endearing moments! He is that enigmatic kind of young man who will intrigue the smart girls, but go unnoticed by the others, who thankfully, will be completely unappreciative of all he has to offer. I love him so much and will miss him tremendously when he leaves for Nashville in the fall. In just a few short weeks.

"I'm sorry, Susannah. I didn't mean to leave Stan out. He was the best of all of us," says Casey, giving me her vulnerable and sweet look that I've only seen a few times since I've known her. I'm touched and humbled simultaneously.

"It's all right. And yes, he was the best, wasn't he?" We are quiet again. Each of us picks a place on the table to ponder while we contemplate Stan's absence in our lives. Maggie gives me a brave smile and a wink, and she covers my hand with hers, giving it a squeeze. In a moment, our server appears to collect our empty plates, offering dessert, which we robustly decline.

Myers looks ready to go, and Casey catches his vibe. They are excited to begin their new adventure together, and ready to be shed of their doting mothers. So we sign our checks with a flourish and leave the restaurant, walking briskly up the sidewalk on Trade Street toward the parking garage, in hopes of countering the effects of our overindulgences at Sweet Potatoes. The mid-day heat and humidity, however, only exacerbate the results of our overeating, and the three of us women groan in shared regret as we trudge along with Myers, who leads the way, unaffected by his caloric intake, hands shoved deep in his pockets, looking around at all the new shops and places a new city has to offer.

It was on a day just like this when he fell in love with Nashville, and I remember the night we'd spent during his Belmont University tour there, strolling up and down the city streets in heat such as this, listening to the buskers playing their music on every street corner, and pausing at open doorways of bars where new music floated out to us. He was too young to go inside some of the places, but he could have held his own with any of the musicians. Stars in the making were a dime a dozen there so I'd thought the sheer numbers of them would intimidate my son, but it had the opposite effect, igniting him, making him want to insert himself into the midst of this musical circus all the more. Once, after Stan and I had taken him to a Mark O'Connor concert, Myers had decided his career path immediately. *I want to be a session violinist*, he'd said. I could imagine him right at home, playing with other artists in a recording studio or in any one of the cafes and bars in Nashville, with his violin, fiddling along by ear with any of them, or out there on the sidewalks, going solo and busking on a corner, his violin case filling with folding money as he worked his magic on the masses. I'd thought Carnegie Hall was where he belonged, and maybe he will land there at some point in his life, but in his mind, the Grand Ole Opry is his mecca. Myers has a unique ability to embrace a variety of musical genres for one so young. While most kids his age are listening to Bruno Mars and One Direction, Myers is studying old videos of eclectic violinist Mark O'Connor on YouTube, and emulating Jason Fitz, the violin/fiddle player from The Band Perry.

In what seems like no time, Maggie has parked in front of the dorms at the North Carolina School of the Arts where Myers and Casey have to check in at the registration desk. I stand in the warm breeze as Myers unloads the luggage and their instruments. Feeling the need to be inconspicuous, I stand behind Myers, letting him take over while he checks in with the staff. "Myers Morgan," he says to an older girl who looks through a box filled with packets for the one with his name, finds it, and hands it to him.

"Room 323, Myers. Third floor," she says beaming up at him.

"Thank you," he says, shouldering his bag, managing his shirts on hangers, and picking up his violin case.

Casey already has her packet and tucks it neatly into her tote bag. One of the volunteers takes her extra bags and offers to help carry them to her room. I want to see Myers's room, but something tells me I should hang back and let him do this on his own. Maggie must be feeling the same thing, I think, as we exchange melancholy looks. We say our goodbyes. Then, with little show of emotion, and hugs for Maggie and me, Myers and Casey are off on their next adventure. Despite the large pink cello case she has slung over one shoulder, and the dresses she carries over one arm, Casey bumps him playfully with her hip, giggling as they walk down the hall toward the elevators. They don't even look back.

Chapter 4

TAKING NOTES

I must be working out all my ambivalent feelings today on our touring and shopping adventure, in what Maggie calls "retail therapy." Already I have bought a pair of earrings for myself, a purse for Mom's birthday present, a new summery fragrance, and some little bars of scented soap for my guest bathroom and some for Maggie. She buys lavender-scented bubble bath while I peruse the greeting cards for a card for Mom, trying to imagine taking the time to soak luxuriously in a warm sweet-smelling bath. I never wanted to waste the water, but I suppose it might be nice to give it a whirl. It's one of those indulgences, like getting a massage, that I should try, especially the hot stone massages that Maggie swears by, so I add it to the list for later—when I'm by myself in the fall. *Killing time.*

Killing time for what? Stan never liked that expression. There is never time to kill when there are warm breezes blowing, luring one out of doors for a walk or a picnic, or when there is a long soaking rain on a cold day, perfect for curling up with a good book and a cup of tea in front of the fire. No need to kill a single moment. Thank you, I think to myself, appreciative again of his wisdom. I wait for him to speak to me, but there is nothing, maybe because Maggie is beckoning me outside. Suddenly, I want to be by myself so I can listen to him.

We leave the chill of the shop's air conditioning, emerging again into the moist summer heat, almost unbearable at this hour, but I choose to ignore my discomfort by enjoying the flowers, baskets, and pots of colorful petunias and nasturtiums, settled in lush green creeping Jenny, cheerily holding their faces up to be admired. It is time to check into our hotel and have a refreshing drink. We've toured the impressive architecture and art treasures inside the Reynolda House Museum, home of Richard Joshua Reynolds, founder of the local R.J. Reynolds tobacco company that bears his name, wandered through the gardens, and have indulged ourselves on frivolities from the gift shop. Despite my comfortable sandals, my feet hurt, swollen with the heat and all the walking we've done. I thought I was in better shape. *Am I getting old?*

Maggie cranks up the air conditioning in the car as we drive to the historic Brookstown Inn. "Whew! I didn't think it would be this hot today!" she exclaims as the air blows her hair away from her face. Turning AC vents toward my own face, I feel the warm air gradually cooling as we glide back onto the street, returning to the downtown area.

"I know! I'll be ready for a cool glass of white wine; how about you?"

"Oh, yes!"

"I brought some in my cooler. I hope it's still cold."

"Wonderful! Cheers! We're empty-nesters again for another two weeks!"

"Yep. Cheers!" I laugh.

Maggie sighs, turning down the air now that it is properly chilled.

"I've been saving this for now. You'll never guess what I found in Casey's drawer yesterday when I was putting her laundry away."

I look apprehensively at her. "What?"

"*Condoms!*"

"No!"

"Yes! And guess where she got them?"

It takes one look at her face to know. "Myers?"

"Yes!" she says, eyes as wide as dinner plates. I blink at her and then we burst out laughing.

"No! You are *kidding!*"

"No, I'm not. But I have to say, as off-balance as I was thrown, we had a great talk about it."

"About sex?"

"Oh, yes. I have to admit, I really can't remember the conversation we had about the birds and the bees when she was about eight, but I obviously didn't cover then what she wanted to know about last night!"

"Oh...my God! What did y'all talk about? Has she *had* sex?"

"No. And Myers hasn't either, to answer your next question."

I breathe a sigh of relief. I *think* I am relieved. It's been years since Myers and I have discussed human reproduction. And that was about as personal as it was. There was a conversation recently that involved my big two rules: never have unprotected sex and never get into a car with a driver who's been drinking. But Stan came to my rescue with Myers on the sex topic as well.

"Oh, thank God...I guess! So what did she ask you?"

"Oh! All kinds of stuff, to shave or not to shave—*down there*—because all of her friends are doing it, and like...what an orgasm feels like, and isn't sex messy? And how to clean yourself up, and how a guy could ever stand to wear a condom!"

We are both hooting with laughter, but I am feeling uneasy about the topic at the same time.

"She wanted to know the etiquette for asking a guy to produce one, and then how to give him one if he wasn't prepared!"

"Oh, that is so honest! What do you suppose prompted all of her curiosity?"

"It's because of the acting. She feels the need to immerse herself in other people's characters so completely now. She was watching a movie with a sex scene and wondered how she'd play the part, not ever having had sex."

"Oh, wow! How in the world did you handle it?"

"We immediately went into the kitchen so I could have a glass of wine!"

"Uh, yeah! I'd have to have one, too."

"I know, and since we were having such an adult conversation, I gave her a sip—or two. It ended up being really sweet. We talked about being in love and how sex can be really special when you're in love. She said she'd heard from other girls that it's fine, too, when you don't love the guy, but she isn't sure she wants to risk being that vulnerable with a guy she doesn't love."

"Oh, that's smart. She's so level-headed! Is there a guy?"

"I don't think so. She's met lots of new guys in her summer programs, but they're really not her type. And I guess she's not theirs...." It's her weight again. Ironically, Myers has acne; Casey is heavy. I'm sure they see their imperfections as curses, but I see them as saving graces, and as my mother used to call them, 'character-building experiences!' If they were too beautiful, they'd be in far over their heads with too many adult decisions to make.

"So Myers gave her the condoms? I didn't know he had them, but it doesn't surprise me."

"Why? Has he fallen for someone?"

"No, not that I'm aware of, but Stan talked to him about all that stuff the summer Myers was thirteen."

"And he wasn't even Myers's father."

"I know, but it was Stan's way to pick up a lot of Kent's slack," I say, gazing out the window at the buildings and storefronts we are passing, like background music in an elevator. People in business attire walk briskly down the sidewalks, heading home from work, talking on cell phones, some checking their watches, while others stroll languidly along, fanning themselves and shading their eyes as they wait at sunny street corners for traffic to stop. Everyone looks hot and uncomfortable. But I hardly take it in.

"I can't believe it's been three years, Susannah."

"I know." We memorialize the event with a moment of silence, and then she can contain her curiosity no longer. "Well, what did they talk about? Did Stan tell you what he told Myers? I mean, how did it come up?"

"Bad pun!"

"Ha!"

"Stan told me all about it. One Saturday morning, Myers went to him, after having his first wet dream. They'd discreetly changed his sheets and started the washing machine while I was out for my morning run. Stan explained what having wet dreams was all about, and they talked about erections and how boys call them 'hard-ons.' He told Myers about making sure when he's ready to have sex that he is responsible enough to buy his own condoms and use them. And not to keep the same one in his pocket for a year! They *do* have a shelf life, he told Myers!"

"Wow! Do you think Kent ever had that kind of conversation with Myers?"

"Pfft! I really doubt it. Kent usually runs the other way at the first sign of confrontation. However...they did have a major powwow last night over their campfire about what all happened with us, but sex? I doubt it. No, Stan and Myers discussed it all. Aside from the responsibility he needs to exercise for the purposes of avoiding pregnancy and STDs, Stan told Myers that sex is a wonderful thing, but it has to be mutual. He told him not to take something away from a girl that he can't give back; that 'no' means '*no*,' and if a girl is even the least bit hesitant, that means 'no,' too, and he should respect that. And that when sex is mutual, it should be mutually satisfying as well, and that he should do whatever it takes to make a girl feel comfortable and cherished. *Loved.* Loved most of all. Wait for love if he can. And then sex will be the most wonderful gift there is between a man and a woman."

Maggie looks at me as she stops the SUV in our parking place in the hotel parking lot. She is blinking. My friend tears up easily, while I, on the other hand, haven't cried in three years.

"Oh, Suz, that's really sweet." She sighs, and I smile at her. "So Myers is waiting?"

"Apparently. I hope so. And Casey? Maybe he and Casey have talked this all out as well. Do you think?"

"I don't know," she says. "Maybe it's just because nobody's shown an interest in her. For whatever reason, I'm glad they're waiting."

"Well, God love Stan. It's a good thing Myers felt comfortable talking to him about those kinds of personal things. He was a remarkable man."

I nod, waiting to hear him tell me something, make a comment, but there is nothing. *Maybe he's embarrassed,* now that I've unloaded all that personal information on Maggie! We sit in the car another moment until the heat makes it unbearable. "Let's go get that glass of wine, shall we?"

"Absolutely."

⁂

At dinner, Maggie and I have still not run out of things to talk about. She is a photographer and graphic designer and wants me to model for an upcoming book cover she's designing. Between that, working at Dream Weavers, our local art gallery, and her interest in music, Maggie is busier than most women I know. She chews gracefully, even as she talks.

"So the story is about a woman who works for a man over the Internet, and they have only a virtual relationship. She jokingly calls him the Wizard of Oz because he's rather intimidating, even though she's never met him face-to-face, and so the book is called *Working for the Wizard*. So, I'm imagining having you posed, standing in front of the tall glass doors on one of the skyscrapers uptown, with your back to the camera, dressed in a little black dress, with red stilettos, and carrying one of those primitive Halloween witches' brooms, you know, like when Dorothy had to bring the Wizard the Wicked Witch's broom? Wouldn't it be a *hoot?*"

"Yes! I love it. And when do you want to do this?" She takes another bite of her Wiener schnitzel as she ponders her schedule.

"Are you free next Saturday? Or...hey, we can do it any evening, now that our brood has flown the coop—for at least the next two weeks."

"Sure. It would be cooler in the evenings."

"And the light would be better—it's the magic time, the hour just before sunset."

"So...I guess I need to buy some red shoes."

"Just go somewhere cheap." She looks up, eyes sparkling with another brilliant idea. "Or not! Get some nice ones that you can wear again!" She laughs out loud.

I laugh too. "Like the proverbial bridesmaid's dress I'll never wear again! Ha! Red stilettos. Right."

"You could, you know. Wear them again." Her eyes are still sparkling.

I know where this thread of conversation is going to lead. She is glancing at my wedding band. It's unusual, a wide band that looks like three in one, with a square diamond in the center. Stan picked it out and had our minister quote Ecclesiastes when he'd put it on my finger: '*A cord of three strands is not easily broken.*' No kidding. My ring doesn't really look like most wedding rings, but I suppose, like the clothes I keep in Stan's closet, others think it's strange that I still wear it.

I look at her, knowing what she's thinking.

"You could have some hot dates with some red shoes, you know?"

I chortle at the thought of all the men I've met lately. Zero. That's one thing Magnolia Village is good for—living small. If I don't want to date, there is certainly no pressure in a place like our village.

"And if I don't want any hot dates, I can save money on shoes, apparently."

She smiles. "Touché. But seriously, after so long, is it getting any easier? Missing Stan, I mean?"

I have to think about how to respond, even with Maggie. "I still miss him terribly. But I'm not sad anymore. I'm becoming more comfortable just being by myself. I have my house just the way I like it, and I guess I've become set in my ways. I don't want anyone else fouling up my system, you know?"

"Maybe it's because you haven't met anybody you like yet."

"Maybe it's because I haven't met *anybody*. I mean, some of the old men who come into my office hit on me in that innocent, playful way that we all know means nothing. I'm glad there are no opportunities for my friends to try and fix me up. But I'm not broken, so I don't need fixing, and frankly, dating terrifies me. I'd feel funny having to turn down anyone, so thank God there's no one beating down my door." I shudder at my own imagination. "Oohh," I say, shaking my head, making Maggie laugh.

"Well...Magnolia is a safe place to live, then. I guess there aren't a lot of men our age who'd be available."

"And if they are, they're guys like Kent—divorced and rightly so. Or *married*...."

This time it is Maggie who shudders. "Oohh!"

We giggle.

"How is *Kent*, by the way?"

"As arrogant as ever. Still dating my sister. Or I should say, still gracing her with his presence."

I think back on my days in medical school at UNC where I met Kent, who was a law student there. We'd met at a bar in Chapel Hill with mutual friends. What had attracted me to him in the first place? His intelligence was obvious, which I later realized was tainted with superiority. His self-confidence was attractive at first too, but later, it morphed into unattractive arrogance. At first I liked his dry sense of humor, but it also eroded—into deep-seated sarcasm. He was truly a fun guy at parties, but it soon became apparent that he was a functioning alcoholic. His distinguished good looks were feeding his narcissism, the combination of which now turns my stomach at the sight of him.

"Why doesn't she dump him?"

"Well…she doesn't know him as well as you'd expect. Jen and I lived in different cities back then, so they weren't around each other all that much when Kent and I were married. He can be charming at first. He wines and dines her and she likes that. Jen is more insecure than she lets on. She makes herself available and he likes it. Now that her children are out of the picture and off her payroll, she and Kent can do whatever they want. But as I've said a million times, she broke the sibling code by getting involved with him in the first place. My feelings in the whole scheme are completely irrelevant to either of them."

"That's so weird. How do her kids react to him?"

"Not favorably. We never hear from Sloan. She's kind of odd…different. She's still in New York, working as a full-figure model and rarely comes home."

"Casey met her, last spring, remember?"

"Oh, that's right. I'd forgotten. That was the last time Sloan was here. Remember Jen's fiftieth birthday party? Wow! Sloan got so mad at Jen because Kent was there that she *left the party!*"

"Oh, I remember that! See, she must have some sense! Myers went after her and he took her with him to see Casey's show."

"*South Pacific*. That's right. I forgot about that, too. Myers wanted to be at the play anyway, and not at Jen's party," I say, taking a sip of my white wine. It's heavenly, and I'm glad the focus is off me again. "And then there's Trip—he's living in Georgia now, working on a shrimp boat near Savannah. He's out of college and probably won't ever come back home."

"What was his major, again?"

"Alcoholism—with a minor in frat parties." We laugh again, but it's really not funny. "I'm sorry. He was a business major. You know, it's a shame that Jen's relationships have mostly ended up in failure, including ours, and it isn't hard to understand why. Still, I miss my sister at times."

"Well, Kent hasn't helped your situation. He should have his head examined."

"Oh, I agree. But there's nothing to be done about it."

I know Kent stands in the way of my relationship with Jen, but even before he came back around, I've always had to work so hard at staying close to my sister—harder than she's been willing to try, and it frustrates me. She closes herself off from so many things in her life that could be good for her. I don't know why. I've often wondered whether being genetically unrelated put us at a disadvantage as siblings. My parents wondered too, but at least I am close to them. And they think Myers hung the moon, so as long as he's around, I'll have all the attention I want from my parents.

Maggie takes her turn in the bathroom to soak in her new lavender bubble bath. She told me I was next, so I unpack my things and discover the gift that's waiting for me at the bottom of my bag. Mom. Listening to Maggie humming one of her favorite folk songs, I pour the other half of my share of white wine, make myself comfortable sitting Indian-style on my bed, and remove the raffia tie and paper, revealing a small coffee-table photo book entitled *Stan the Man,* as Myers used to call him. I gasp, understanding immediately my mother's timely tribute to her favorite son-in-law. As I slowly turn each page, I uncover photo after photo that one of us took with Stan, a sweet trip down memory lane. There is the photo she took of him with Myers and me at the hospital when they rescued us the night of our car accident—that illuminating night that started my relationship with Stan. There are photos of us at a picnic at my parents' house, then at my house with the Frenchs, a photo of Stan holding his guitar and Myers with my violin, the first time we'd realized they could play music together. There are more photos: Stan and Myers at Myers's first violin recital, then the three of us at a soccer game. I'm giving Myers a high five for "getting back on the horse" and playing soccer again after his injury. It was a horse he eventually grew tired of, but nonetheless, he was no quitter. There are pictures of our wedding day, the casual beach ceremony we had on the deck of an opulent beach house we rented for our families at Isle of Palms in June of that year. The pictures go on and on—so many great memories from the eight years I had with Stan. I find myself smiling more and more, so pleased with my mother's thoughtfulness and that she has made and given me this treasure. A tear slides down the side of my nose as I turn the last page—my father, Stan, and me at Stan's fifty-first birthday, three days before he died. Tears are flowing freely now, and I wipe them prudently away before they can damage my new favorite thing. I sit as still as possible on the bed, waiting to hear his voice again, to feel his arms around me as I always have...but there is nothing.

I hear the bathroom door open and Maggie's happy voice as she emerges in a cloud of lavender-scented steam.

"Next!" she sings out to me.

Chapter 5

RED SHOES

It is raining again this evening, the third day in a row. I'm sitting at the table in my cheery blue and yellow cottage kitchen with a cup of tea, waiting to be cheered, watching baby robins in their nest outside my kitchen window. They are silent for a moment, and then as if on cue, all three of them pop up at once, opening their large yellow beaks and crying out to be fed. Their mother is there instantaneously, jamming worms down their throats, silencing them while she goes in search of more. There should be plenty of worms floating to the surface of the ground today. The downpour that began at noon hasn't let up since. I sigh heavily. Rain....

My mind wanders to another rainy day about eleven years ago when Stan and I first met for coffee, the first time we'd met and talked privately after the beer bottle incident and my wreck. It was the day our lives changed so suddenly. When he'd called me one night to check on us and I'd informed him I'd filed for divorce, he'd really stepped up his game, inviting me out for coffee immediately. Under the circumstances, I would normally have been reluctant to meet another man so early in my resolve to dump my husband, but Stan had been on my mind in more ways than I wanted to admit. He'd been so patient with me during our conversations that were becoming more and more personal, and he'd sounded so adamant on the phone that we needed to talk. Sitting with him in the coffee shop, there was an electrical charge in the air between us that had nothing to do with the lightning outside. Myers was spending the afternoon at Tim's, so I'd allowed myself to escape with Stan for the better part of two hours. Our conversation had covered everything imaginable about our lives up until then, almost as if paving the way for the inevitable intimacy we were headed for. I'd lost myself completely, staring unabashedly and dreamily into his face, propping my chin on my hand, captivated by his accent and the sensuality he exuded. In the hospital, I knew he was kind; you expect doctors to be caring, but here in the coffee shop, he was warm and unpretentious and even better-looking than I remembered. I felt myself falling for him in spite of myself.

"So how did you end up in the States?" I'd asked.

"My mother'd attended university here on an exchange program and gotten really enamored of her host family. When my dad left us, they were the people she'd gravitated to, so she plucked me up and off we went. I followed in her footsteps, became a doctor, and…been here ever since," he'd said, eyes softening at me. "But even *I* didn't *really* know why—until now."

"Now? Why now?" I asked, realizing that his hand was covering mine. He rubbed the back of it with his thumb and thought a moment. He hesitated, then looked me in the eyes.

"Because, love, I think I was supposed to meet *you*," he said, lifting my hand to kiss it. "It certainly took you long enough to appear! But I knew after you showed up in my ER the second time, you were meant for me and not that arse of a man you're married to!"

A slow grin spread across my face. He had me at that very moment. I'll always remember it.

Now I sit here, sighing, listening to the rain beating on the roof, remembering how the sound of it used to cheer me when I'd lie in Stan's arms, thinking of that day, but today it just makes me miss him even more.

Talk to me.

Maggie and I were supposed to shoot the cover photograph in front of the Duke Energy Building this evening, but we'd cancelled due to the rain, and the ridiculous red shoes sit in my tote bag by the door, waiting for their debut. Maybe it is just as well. I'm not in the mood to pretend to be pretty today. So here I sit, warming my hands around my favorite blue and white mug, filled with steaming orange tea, wondering what salad I'll fix for supper. It's hard cooking for one person, so salads are my go-to meal these days.

I miss Myers more than ever, and I miss cooking for him. Peeling potatoes for a growing soon-to-be man apparently gave me more pleasure than I realized. My independent son has texted me periodically, letting me know all is well and that he's having a ball at camp, but I miss our talks. He made me laugh. I miss his silent presence as well. Just knowing he was in his room doing homework or playing his violin was comforting. I am suddenly envious of my mother robin, who has returned with more worms. Does she even know how lucky she is? What is my purpose now? I'm no longer a wife and now motherhood is slipping through my fingers.

It was an equally depressing day at the office. I always hate telling someone her melanoma has returned. I had to do it today. The young woman I have treated over the past few years had no clue how devastating my news was going to be, and she hadn't thought to bring anyone with her to help absorb the blow. Damn these tanning beds! If I could outlaw them tomorrow, I would. People have no idea how dangerous they are.

I sip my tea, my thoughts turning to my friend Patti Chase. The only thing harder than delivering that kind of news is delivering it to a friend. Detective Andrew Chase's wife, Patti, was in the same boat. I remember the day I told her that her melanoma had returned. She hadn't brought her husband with her, either. I expected her to dissolve in a pool of tears, as so many patients do, but she held it together bravely. Or maybe she was just in shock, as some of them are, and it didn't sink in at first. But I'll never forget her reaction. It was not what I expected at all. For whatever reason, she was clearly thinking of *me*. She'd leaned across my desk and placed her hand over mine, her pale blue eyes looking into mine, and said, "Don't worry about me, Susannah. I've got Chase. He's the absolute best. He'll take care of me. You did everything you could."

That was over two years ago. She lasted three months and was gone. Patti was one of the first people I met in Magnolia. Stan and I met her when we opened our joint checking account at her bank. She told me about her Pilates class and invited me to join. I didn't know her extremely well, but we saw each other once or twice a week. We talked at the beginning and the end of every class, as busy women sometimes do, wishing to get to know each other better. She was so proud of her family and talked about them quite a bit, especially her husband. Then she became my patient and her death hit me especially hard.

After Patti died, her daughter, Olivia, a lovely red-haired, eighteen-year-old girl, took her mother's message to the public and gave a speech to her high school that spring before she graduated. *Tanning Beds Are Bad*, was the name of her campaign, and she came to my office one day and convinced me to help her. She and I went to every high school that would have us to deliver our message. She told her mother's story of regular visits to tanning beds to get that enviable summer tan that eventually killed her. *Vanity is not worth your life*, she said. *And besides, the vampire look is in!* That quip always got a laugh, with the plethora of vampire books and movies our young audience was doubtlessly consuming. I thought Olivia was brilliant. Who would forget that line? My part in the presentation was to give the statistics and my experiences from a doctor's point of view. *Skin cancer is real, and even if you don't think you have it now, chances are, if you are tanning, in a bed, by the pool, or on the beach, you will have an increased risk*, I told them. We gave out hundreds of sunscreen applicators, the little spray-on wands like the ones handed out at golf tournaments. My practice and Patti's bank donated them.

It was exhausting, both physically and emotionally, but one of the best things I've ever done. I felt even closer to Patti after she died, perhaps vicariously through Olivia. I never knew Detective Chase, apart from paying my condolences at Patti's funeral, except for once, after her initial diagnosis, when he'd come into my office with a spot he was worried about under his left sideburn. It was a small lesion I'd removed that proved to be a basal cell carcinoma, requiring more invasive surgery.

"It's small, but I thought I should get it checked," he shrugged as I pushed his hair away from his face with my thumb to get a better look. I ran fingers through his short hair, somewhere between sandy and ginger-colored, checking his scalp for further lesions. He was probably a cute, red-headed little boy, I remember thinking.

"You were right to come in and get it checked out. Small can be big." Of course he would know this. It was hard to look at him or talk to him and not be consumed with my memories of Patti. "And lots of lesions tend to be on the left side. It's from driving. Most people, especially in professions like yours, who drive a lot, have more sun exposure to their left sides," I continued, examining the rest of his face, neck, and his arms and hands as well. He has the pinkish-fair and freckled complexion of most redheads, turned ruddy by his age and sun exposure, and I made him promise to use sunscreen from there on out. He must have complied, and thankfully for him, I haven't seen him in my office since.

I've finished my tea and the mother robin has gone again. I can't bear to hear her little ones cry out for food, so I move into the living room. The news should be on, so I switch on the TV, wondering when this rain will stop, when the shoes in the tote bag catch my eye.

Why not?

Thinking I would meet Maggie for our photo shoot after work, I'm wearing my black dress, the A-line sleeveless shift with the ballet neck that I wear to everything from work, to dinner out, to cocktail parties. It's the perfect little black dress that every woman has in her closet. It can be dressed up or down with the right accessories. I take the shoes out of their box and hold the back of the couch for balance as I slip my feet awkwardly into one and then the other. I walk around to view myself in the full-length mirror of my antique wardrobe, a large oak piece Stan and I found that reportedly came from England.

A giddy laugh escapes my lips at the sight of my long legs in these red patent leather pumps. I actually don't look half-bad. My morning runs and Pilates classes have done fine work on my legs. I stand a moment, waiting for a comment from Stan. He'd love this. I can imagine his eyes popping the way they did when I dressed—or undressed—in front of him, or gave him a certain provocative pose. But there is nothing. I have had nothing from Stan since the day Myers and I left for Winston-Salem.

Come on! I call to him inwardly, giving him my best pose, impatient with him for leaving me alone.

Alone. I am alone, and I don't like it. Normally on a day like today, I would sit down at my piano and play lovely Debussy rainy-day songs, or something jazzy and upbeat to elevate my mood, but I haven't touched the keys in over a week. I feel deserted. Betrayed. Lonely.

I need a book to read. The weatherman on TV drones on about the rain that is projected to last over the five-day forecast. Okay, a big book. I check my look again, trying to imagine standing in front of the imposing skyscraper doors with a witch's broom in my hands. I attempt to click my heels together as Dorothy did, while murmuring, "There's no place like home," but the heels make it impossible—especially on this rug. Forget it, then. I toe off the shoes and return them to their box and their tote bag, eager to change into shorts and a comfortable shirt for the remainder of my solitary evening.

That achieved, I busy myself in the kitchen, boiling an egg, slicing a green apple, preparing my spinach salad, and pondering which book I haven't read when the phone rings.

The caller ID tells me it is my sister. Glory be!

"Hey, Jen! What's up?"

"I'm out in this crap and wondered if I could stop by. You home for a while?"

"Yeah...just fixing a salad for dinner. Want to join me?"

There is no answer while the thought of a salad falls flat on Jen's end of the phone.

"Nah, I don't think so, but if you're eating, do you mind if I just hang out and have a drink with you for a bit?"

"Uh...I wasn't planning on a drink, but sure, stop by."

"Okay. See you in a few," she says and ends the call. Something is up. It is not like my sister just to pop by.

Within minutes, she is at my door.

"Come on in!" I call as I run the hard-boiled egg under cold water before peeling it.

"Hey!" she calls back, leaving her umbrella propped on the front porch, coming to me and giving me a hug. I wonder whether this is about Stan. She usually doesn't honor the anniversary of his passing the way the rest of us do. I doubt it occurs to her at all.

"Hey! What are you doing out in this mess?"

"Ha! Can you believe some poor guy's wife dragged him out in this rain to look at a property? I hate it when people do that. They show up in front of a house they like and call you up on their cell phones like you're completely available."

"But you agreed to show them?"

"Well, I was on my way home from the office so I figured, 'What the hell?'"

"You could have *lied* and said you were indisposed." It's a dig I should be ashamed of, but I'm not. My sister is the consummate liar, as her ex-husband can attest. She shoots me a look. I know she needs the sale, so no matter the inconvenience, she would avail herself in a heartbeat.

"I figured anybody desperate enough to call me out in this kind of weather might be a serious buyer."

"And were they?"

"Maybe. They seemed really interested, but you never know."

"What property?"

"It's that cute little bungalow over on Bluebell."

I know the one. The yard is adorable with a butterfly garden the owners have planted, and there's a swing.

"The one with the little swing hanging from a tree in the front yard?"

"That's the one. And they loved the gardens, so we'll see. You're really not having a drink?"

"We could open some wine. Or do you want a beer?" I know she wants a gin and tonic, but I'm not equipped to meet her needs.

"Wine sounds good."

"Red all right? I have white, but it's not chilled."

"Sure," she says, seating her voluptuous self at my kitchen island and making herself at home. I go to the wine rack and select a moderately priced red blend and set it and the wine tool in front of her. She should know where I keep the glasses.

I go back to peeling my egg and watch her settle herself into the task of uncorking the bottle. My sister is curvy where I am straight, with lovely honey-colored skin that she cultivates to perfection in a deck chair by the Magnolia Community Swimming Pool every chance she gets. Her thick tawny hair is pulled back into a sleek short ponytail, exposing small gold earrings that match her chunky bracelet. She's wearing a pale yellow blouse and dark brown crop pants in that nice, professional dress of the real estate agent, completed with the essential designer flats in a color that "pops." Her matching orange handbag is perched on the end of the island, and she's looking helplessly at me since I've supplied no glasses.

"Cabinet right behind you, over the wine rack."

"Oh. Okay," she says, retrieving two glasses. I've finished preparing my salad and we go to the kitchen table where she can watch me eat.

She pours my wine, thinking about what she is going to say to me. I can't wait.

"Kent said he had a great time camping with Myers."

I knew it. She's on a mission for my ex.

"Yeah, Myers enjoyed it. He said Kent killed a copperhead."

She nods, evidently having heard the same story.

"Cheers," she says, and we raise our glasses. Here it comes.

I chew as she continues. "I really want us all to be friends, Susannah. It's so difficult with all the tension in the air."

"Go figure that one," I say, unable to help myself.

"Can we pleeease just bury the hatchet?"

"Myers is going to college in less than two months, Jen. There's no need to keep up appearances. What did Kent say? Does this have something to do with their talk on the camping trip?"

"It doesn't have anything to do with Myers. I really wish you could get along with Kent. And I'd just like to be friends with you again."

"I'd really like that, too, Jen." Just not with Kent in the picture.

I watch her for a moment. I can't help thinking about the time I realized Kent was into her, and I have to stifle a laugh. I'd gotten Rascal Flatts concert tickets for Myers's sixteenth birthday. I'd bought them for Jen and myself, and Myers and his friend Tim, but Kent found out about it and decided he'd buy a ticket and come along. He was always jealous of the stuff I did with Myers, especially when it involved music. I didn't care. I had finally become able to tolerate Kent in a small crowd at that point. Maggie and Casey had tickets too, so we all decided to make a real party out of the event. It was all fine and good fun until we were at our seats in the outdoor amphitheater and Jen started dancing. Other people were dancing too, but she was definitely outstanding. She has this Egyptian-like, creepy style of dancing that didn't really fit with the country-rock style of Rascal Flatts. After a couple of beers, she was slowly undulating all over. In her short-shorts and emerald green camisole that showed her navy blue bra straps, she was a real sight. Maggie and I were noticing her odd dance moves, along with the rest of the crowd around us. Even Myers and Tim were snickering as she waved and turned her hands like snakes in the air, as if she were Salome, dancing for John the Baptist's head. It was weird, but Jen was completely uninhibited in her zone. The only person who appreciated her moves other than for humor's sake was Kent. And he was right in the zone with her. They'd gotten along okay before, being in-laws forced upon each other, but that night, the sparks were really flying between them. They've been an item ever since.

And now she is fighting for his self-esteem. How nauseating. And if he knew, he'd kill her!

"So you're saying bury the hatchet?"

"Uh-huh," she nods.

"But, see…I don't care for him at all. I mean, I know I have to tolerate Kent because he's Myers's father, but I really don't care to socialize with him. Or participate in family gatherings with him—with you."

"But family get-togethers are sooo *awkward!*" she wails.

"Yes, they are. I predicted all of this. Remember?"

"You know Mom and Dad would be so much happier if everyone got along."

"Uh—I think Mom and Dad are in my camp on this one," I say warily. "Why are you bringing this up now?"

"Well...it just might be that one day, Kent really will be back in the family, so we'll have to adjust, you know?"

I freeze. Surely not. "Have you got *news* to tell me?"

"Not yet, but I think it's only a matter of time."

"Oh...so you think that when Myers goes off the grid, Kent will propose?"

I feel the urge to gulp my red wine, so I do. She takes a delicate sip.

"Maybe. If it is the case, I want you to be comfortable with it."

I try not to roll my eyes for her dignity's sake. "Jen...you and Kent should have thought about this a long time ago. It's not a problem any of us should have." She says nothing but regards me with those all-knowing eyes. What? What does she know?

"Have you talked about marriage with Kent? Do you really think he's good at it?"

It dawns on me that even after Kent's talk with Myers, he could have changed his mind about not getting married again.

Then she gives me her most piteous look and says what every seven-teen-year-old girl says about the notorious bad boy she's hot for. "Kent's changed, Susannah. I think you should give him another chance...with me, that is. For my sake. Can you do that?"

How utterly condescending! Is she for real? It's not even worth dis-cussing. Does she really think he's okay? It takes every bit of restraint I have to say, "I promise to conduct myself properly should the occasion arise." I shouldn't say another word.

"It will be important for you to try not to keep one-upping Kent if he does plan to marry me."

Holy cow! She really said the "m" word. But what is she talking about?

"How am I one-upping Kent?" I am truly puzzled.

"Sending Myers off to Belmont is a bit emasculating, don't you think?"

Belmont University costs upwards of $30,000 a year in tuition and I didn't ask Kent to contribute a dime. I can afford it. Myers wanted to go there. End of story. Stan and I talked about Belmont when Myers became such an accomplished musician and we both thought he should be able to live his dream.

"I can do it for Myers without having to ask Kent."

"He thinks you're spoiling Myers."

"That's ridiculous. Besides, it wasn't me who bought him a brand new SUV for his sixteenth birthday, which he immediately wrecked."

Jen stares me down evenly. "No. That probably wasn't a good idea."

"Besides, Kent went to law school and is living his dream. Why shouldn't Myers get to do the same thing? He's my only child. Kent doesn't have to worry about a thing."

She can't think of a comeback, so she lifts her hand in defeat. "Fine. Whatever. I just don't want it to make you unhappy if Kent and I get married," she says, giving me another piteous look.

"I'll be okay," I say, taking a bite of my salad and watching her drink her wine. I really have lost my appetite, but I don't want her thinking she's rattled me.

She looks around my house, the emptiness of it screaming out, and returns her sad eyes to me.

"Are you at least *dating?*"

"Is it a necessity?"

She is staring at my ring. There is no hope for me, the pathetic widow, as long as I'm wearing my wedding ring. I wish I still had on the black dress. I have a sudden urge to put on the red shoes and strut around for her. Maybe I should put on a show so she'll get off my case, but it might actually backfire, and then she'd start in on me about Internet dating. I can't take the thought of that. She hasn't once mentioned Stan and how I might be feeling about his loss three years later. I drink more wine.

"I don't plan on dating—period. I'm okay, really. Now, don't *you* have a date with Prince Charming this evening or something?" I say, making shooing motions at her with my hand.

"Not tonight. He's working on a case."

It's my turn to give her one of my all-knowing looks since her comment makes me remember Kent's late nights with Dirty Penny and all her apparent charms. But I resist the urge to give her the look and smile at her instead. It's time for her to be on her way.

"Thanks for stopping to check on me. I'm good. Really. And I hope you get what you want, Jen."

"Thanks, sweetie," she says, giving me a wink and draining her wine glass. We stand and hug again, and then I walk her to the door where we bid each other goodbye.

I lean against the door for a moment, watching her lift her umbrella and walk to her car, listening to the blip-blip-blop of raindrops that have started up again. I get that she's lonely too, but I hope I'll never be as desperate as to fall for another guy like Kent. I'd much rather be alone. I sigh deeply and walk to the bookcase, still holding my napkin, scanning the titles of books I remember, those I don't, and ones I have yet to read. All the authors—Anita Shreve, Emily Bronte, Rosamunde Pilcher, and John Hart—look back at me like old friends I'd like to visit again. It's just at a moment like this when I'd hear Stan chime in. I'd feel his mouth at my ear, a kiss, and then, *Choose* Wuthering Heights, *baybe,* he'd say. I wait.

But again, there is nothing.

Chapter 6

THREE DEGREES OF DR. BRODY

It's one of those days when I can't help but notice how connected I am to the residents of Magnolia Village. It seems that every third person I have encountered since I left my office has been a patient of mine. I've mastered the art of the friendly greeting without that tell-tale expression on my face that says, *I know all your secrets.* I stopped at the dry cleaner's on my way home. The owner has been under my care numerous times for excision of precancerous lesions. He's fifty-something and has a passion for deep sea fishing, solidifying our relationship for years to come. And then I'm happily greeted by the high school girl who works as a cashier at the market around the corner from my house. I have treated her acne for years and we are both thrilled with the results. She looks so beautiful now!

On the sidewalk as I walk to dinner, I smile and greet a young man whom I used to treat for psoriasis. He's trying a special diet before returning to traditional medication. He desperately wants to date, but girls look away from him as soon as he can strike up a conversation. Now he looks good. Whatever he's doing is working. I support the holistic approach and advise my patients to look at all their options. He smiles shyly and passes me on the sidewalk. My heart aches while I give him his space and say a silent prayer for him. What a great guy. Life can be so unfair.

A cool breeze hints at more rain later this evening as I notice the sky has turned a steely blue. I check my purse, making sure I've remembered to bring my umbrella. Sitting on the porch at The Raw Bar is evidently going to be out, I think, as thunder rumbles faintly in the distance. It's one of my favorite restaurants where I'm meeting Maggie and Barbara Linden. I try not to make more than friendly eye contact with Betty, the hostess. I've injected far too much Botox in her face, but she insists on coming back for more. She looks constantly surprised, and it's hard to tell whether she's smiling or smirking, but she seems happy with the results; however, she's not the worst. The most awkward encounters I have are with the people whom I have treated for genital warts or some other forms of sexually transmitted diseases. Those folks usually run the other way when they see me coming so I don't have to worry about how I'm going to handle myself!

Tonight, I find myself counting...four people in the space of an hour, who have been under my healing hands. I feel the sudden need to become incognito, wishing I'd worn sunglasses and a scarf tied around my head, like Ingrid Bergman or Audrey Hepburn in the old movies! It is, I remind myself, a small town.

I'm first to arrive at the hostess stand, so I practice my most pleasant smile at Botox Betty, who gives me a wink as she leads me to our table. No sooner have I been seated than Barb and Maggie appear with shopping bags in hand. I stand to give them hugs as we exchange greetings.

"How was your visit with your grandchildren? How's the new baby?" I ask Barb, knowing we'll hear many funny stories about what the older ones are saying and doing now, and how adorable her new grandson is. She is about to launch into a story as our waiter appears to take our order. Thankfully, I haven't treated him and we have eaten here so often we don't even need to look at the menu, but we listen politely anyway as he recites the evening specials. We all choose the salmon salads and sip our water. Barb finishes her story and reciprocates her interest.

"Have you missed your own children?" Barb asks. We will be leaving tomorrow to attend their final chamber music concert and bring them home from "camp."

"Oh, yes!" Maggie says. "It seems like Casey's been gone for ages."

"She has," I remind her. "She's been gone most of the summer. So has Myers, and I miss him like crazy."

Barb props her elbow on the table and rests her chin on a hand. "How are you both dealing with being empty-nesters?"

Maggie and I glance at each other, exchanging smiles.

"I sort of like it. I'm adding more and more ideas to my list of things to do when Myers leaves for college. Once he goes, I probably won't see him until Thanksgiving."

"Nashville is pretty far away. Will you fly him home, or go out and visit?"

"I'm sure I'll fly him home. I won't be able to take the time off. Lots of people schedule appointments when they're home over the holidays. It would be nice to go out to visit at Christmas, though."

Holidays, especially Christmas for Myers and me, are different now that Stan is gone. We spend Christmas with my parents and Jen, but with the possibility of Kent's presence looming, I really might have to find an excuse to get out of town!

Maggie is quiet. The talk of traveling with Myers must get her down. Casey would kill for an opportunity like Myers is going to have, and her little jaunt down the highway to college in Columbia seems like small potatoes in comparison.

"Well, I can't wait to hear them perform tomorrow. I've missed not being there. And I'll miss the two of them terribly when they take off for college."

"They'll miss you too, Barb," says Maggie.

"It's a rare thing, you know, to have two such gifted students in one small village. I know I've said it before, but prodigies like Casey and

Myers don't just come along every day. You'll have to be sure and keep me posted on what they're doing. My professional life will certainly be lacking without them around to keep me inspired and entertained!"

The restaurant is starting to get crowded. The waiter returns in record time with our salads. We tuck in immediately as hunger takes over our conversation for a few moments. From our table in the corner, we can see most of the customers coming in, and I have a good view of the oyster bar where a sports channel is broadcasting a pre-game show on a flat screen. My father brought me up on baseball, so I have a genuine interest in who is playing. My horizons expanded past the Atlanta Braves when I met Stan. He was a devout Red Sox fan from the time he lived in Massachusetts with his mother. As I watch to see who is playing to-night, I see Detective Andrew Chase taking a seat at the oyster bar. He has lost the required suit coat and tie of his occupation in the afternoon heat, and his pale green shirt is spattered with dark spots—it's apparently raining again. He runs a hand over his light gingery hair to expel rain-drops and makes himself comfortable at the bar. Alone. He is like me. Maggie and Barb do not notice him; they discuss the cello teacher from the University of South Carolina that Barb knows while I study Chase.

He is number five. Five people I've seen whom I've treated since I left the office today. I'd say I have the corner on the skin care market in the village. Obviously; I'm the only dermatologist here. But Chase is disconcertingly different for me. He settles his arms on the bar, watches the flat screen for a moment, and then stares blankly. I can tell, even by looking at his back, that he is staring at nothing. Then he hangs his head for several moments until the bartender is free. God, I know that dismal feeling. I strain to hear him order a beer and a dozen oysters on the half shell. Dinner and a beer, watch a little baseball, go home to an empty house...just like me.

They were such a solid family, Chase and Patti and their two kids, Olivia and Ryan. Both of them are in college now, and Chase is on his own. He is one of those men you see who looks like he has it all together; smart, good-looking, a good husband, and a great dad. Since I didn't know him personally, I found it intriguing to try and imagine what kind of guy Patti would be married to. I imagined he'd be busy all the time—working, going to his kids' games and concerts, picking up milk at the store, taking his wife out for a date night once a month, and ushering at church on Sunday mornings. And to look at him tonight, you'd think the same thing, except for that hang-dog look that gives him away. *Do I look like that?*

"Susannah?" Barb brings me back into the conversation. I am caught hopelessly daydreaming.

"What? Oh. I'm sorry."

"I was wondering what else Myers has going on this summer before he heads off to college?"

"Oh, you know...doing whatever he can to get out of Magnolia."

"I know, right? Casey is so sick of our little village. It's so strange how our views change over time. When I was her age, I wouldn't have wanted to live in a place like this either. It would be so small and stifling for a young person, but it's exactly the kind of small town atmosphere Ed and I craved after years of living the Chicago rat race. If Ed's brother hadn't relocated to Charlotte, we never would have found this place. The climate and the cost of living and convenience of life here are so much better. I can't imagine where we'd be happier."

"I know. Stan and I felt the same way when we found this place. My parents lured us here, and Magnolia Village was just the little slice of heaven Stan and I needed. I've always loved the peace and quiet. But in answer to your question, Barb, Myers has all kinds of music events he wants to take in before he leaves. The Fiddle and Bow Society has lots of concerts he wants to attend, and he wants to go to some of the summer music festivals before he leaves."

"Don't your children ever just 'hang out' at the pool?"

"I'm sure there will be some of that thrown in and a lake visit or two with Tim's family. They go to Lake Norman so often I don't even blink an eye anymore."

"So...back to the end of chamber music camp. What time should we head out in the morning?" Maggie asks me.

We make our plans for the morning's departure and then Barb asks, "Will Myers's father be at the closing concert?"

I hadn't even thought about Kent. If he knows about the concert, I haven't heard. He normally doesn't attend Myers's music events unless he's asked. It could happen, but I'd be surprised.

"I honestly don't know. Unless Myers has asked him, I doubt he'd be interested enough to leave town for a concert. Kent and I don't talk that much. But...that could all be changing."

"How so?" asks Maggie. I regret instantly that I've opened this can of worms. I haven't told her yet about my conversation with Jen, but I've thought more and more about my sister's ensuing relationship with Kent. So reluctantly, I begin.

"I haven't told you, but Jen came by the other day and said she thinks Kent might be *proposing* to her soon."

Barb chuckles. She knows my history with Kent and, even better, his history with my sister. "Oh, boy! I'll bet that went over like a turd in a punchbowl!"

"Absolutely!" says Maggie, chortling at the idea of their marriage.

"I know...it's like a Shakespearean comedy. It's funny to everyone but me, the main character in this whacky play. And awkward doesn't even come close to describing the whole situation."

"Does she seriously think he'll ask her?" asks Maggie, wide-eyed, wiping her mouth with her napkin.

"Yes, I think she does. Which is really odd because Myers said Kent told him on their camping trip that he'd never get married again, and that he's not 'good at being married.' So either he's had a change of heart or she's really deluding herself."

"Oh, that's not very healthy," says Barb.

Or, he could be lying to Myers, I think to myself, knowing that could be all too true.

"No, it's not healthy at all. If she is deluding herself, then I hate to see my sister get hurt. And I really hate to see Kent—period!"

They laugh and I succeed at steering the conversation away from my odd, in-bred family circumstances by asking what is in their shopping bags. After they've regaled me with the sales they found at our favorite boutique, we all look up as Chase walks past our table. I catch my breath as our eyes meet and both of us freeze for a second. I know it's more than an occupational hazard of his, but he has that look—those deep, penetrating green eyes that make me feel as though he knows exactly what I'm thinking. He seems as caught off-guard as I do, but then he recovers instantly, giving me a little nod and a wave. He mouths, "Hi" and I wave back. He is far enough away that neither of us speaks. My face reddens as my friends follow my gaze.

"Who is that?" asks Barb.

"*That* is Andrew Chase," says Maggie pointedly. "Isn't he *hot?*"

"Why does he look so familiar?"

"You've probably seen him on TV," says Maggie. "He's a detective. Remember last fall when there was that string of robberies on the news? He was interviewed a couple of times about it, and he eventually caught the people responsible. I'm sure you saw it."

"Sounds dangerous. So how do you know him, Susannah?"

"I can tell you because it's common knowledge, but normally I wouldn't say. I treated his wife." *And him.* "She was also a friend of mine. We all used to go to Pilates together," I say, nodding to Maggie.

"She died of melanoma," Maggie supplies. I look down. I have that nagging pang of guilt again that perhaps somehow it was my fault. If Patti had come in earlier, I could have caught her recurrence earlier. I could have saved her. I let that nice family down.

"Oh...how sad. She couldn't have been very old."

"No," I reply. "She was forty-two. It was very sad." And so unnecessary.

My friends make sympathetic noises: *Mmm, Ohhh.*

My eyes drop to the napkin in my lap. Being a doctor, caring for people and relieving their suffering, has allowed me to possess a certain level of satisfaction in my life. Practicing medicine has given me that solid sense of self-worth in relieving a pain, healing a wound, laying a worry to rest. I need that feeling in the same way I need air to breathe. But that feeling was obliterated with Patti Chase, and every time I look at her husband, a man I do not really know, I am reminded of my failure to make her whole. I am reminded that her life slipped through my fingers. It is hard to turn my face toward his wondering moss green eyes, which are instantly filled with emotion upon seeing me—sorrowful emotion, of which I have some inkling.

I clear my throat. My face is burning. Our waiter is back with our checks. I go through the motions of reviewing my check, placing my debit card inside the black folio, and setting it on the edge of the table while a poignant memory flashes again in my mind of eighteen-year-old Olivia Chase, reaching for her dad's hand at the funeral.

I let them *all* down.

Chapter 7

TAKE THAT!

Maggie and I take our seats just as the lights are dimming in the theater. After following our children's musical careers for so many years, there are always many friends we've made along the way to catch up with at these events, so we are late getting seated. Barb has joined her faculty friends near the back of the auditorium, and as I locate her, she gives me a wave and a wink. I narrow my eyes, watching that little Hannah McIntyre dart from the ladies' room, tucking her white blouse into her flared black skirt, and fluffing her dark hair that she's taken the time to style in soft waves around her face. She is even more attractive than I remember, and I can see why Myers was so taken with her last year.

I close my eyes, wishing Stan could witness Myers perform now. Stan, not me, introduced Myers to music. He was the reason Myers took up the violin. He'd suggested that Myers try out my old instrument when Myers was hesitant to play soccer again after his throat healed. I'd never realized Myers could play by ear, and Stan encouraged him from the start to join a group of friends he knew who were into Celtic music. That initial association morphed into yearly pilgrimages to Merle Fest every spring, the annual bluegrass festival Stan never missed in Wilkesboro, North Carolina, in memory of renowned guitarist Doc Watson's son,

Merle. Stan was himself a renowned guitarist and mandolin player in Charlotte, and it was another stroke of destiny that brought Myers and him together.

I listen to the strings warming up behind the curtain and attempt to read my program in the dark, seeing that Myers and Casey are in the first quartet with two Asian students we don't know.

The curtain rises and Maggie and I glance excitedly at each other. Myers looks stunning in his black shirt and glinting silver cuff links as he rises into his pose. Casey settles the cello neatly between her knees, having had the good sense to wear a long black dress. Her hair is pulled loosely into a ponytail, as if an afterthought, when a little makeup and a curling iron might have served her better, but her appearance will go unnoticed once she draws her bow across the strings. She has the impish grin to prove I'm right. And they begin.

Mendelssohn's Quartet in E Major is uplifting and brilliantly played. I watch the musician's eyes as they glance from the pages of their music to each other's faces, swaying with the music, giving their bodies and expressions over to the feelings the melodies and harmonies chase around the room. It is magic, and for a moment, my fiddle-playing son is a classical musician in his own right. There is no doubt in my mind that one day, Carnegie Hall will embrace him with open arms. Casey, with her usual sparkle, continues the musical conversation with him and the others. She could be there, too; of this, I am sure.

A stolen glance at the other audience members confirms my thoughts. And then *finally*, I am warmed instantly and inwardly, a token from Stan that he is *here*, in this place, as proud of Myers as I am. Present. Maybe Myers feels it too as he closes his eyes and loses himself in another world. I'd like to think they still have their connection the way I do with Stan. There is no need for the musical score in front of him. He has memorized this piece, in what, two weeks? However long it has been in front of him, and being the proud parent I am, I am still impressed with his talent. The transcendence for both of us, rather, all *three* of us, ends all too soon, and the audience erupts into enthusiastic applause. *Aren't you proud?* I say to Stan, and I'm rewarded with a warm embrace, but no words.

The four musicians rise and bow before they exit the stage and the next group enters. The teacher introduces the piece, a Tchaikovsky quartet that will be next with other students I don't know. There is a lovely girl, playing violin in this one, with a veil of light brown hair that falls over her cheek as she plays. She is tiny. I wonder whether she eats. She has an intelligent face and exudes a peerless sense of self-confidence. I wonder whether Myers talks to her. She would be my pick for him, I think, as I watch her reaction to the music, her pale skin apparently unacquainted with the sun. In the space of sixteen counts where the violin rests, she tucks her hair behind her ear and gets ready, eyes never leaving the score. She is impeccably dressed in a lacy, short-sleeved blouse and a black skirt she's set off with black tights and ankle-high black boots. What am I thinking? Me, the anti-shopping queen who is suddenly taken in by an on-trend look on a half-starved seventeen-year-old girl? I blink and try to come back to my senses. I feel apologies are necessary to Casey for some reason. The frumpy, under-made-up, yet fascinating Casey French. Who will my son cast his affections upon? Surely, it will not be anyone of my choosing, just as anyone I were to set my eye upon will be no one the masses would certainly pick for me!

The Tchaikovsky piece is over before I have responded the way I should. The performers have left me sadly flat over it, and as they receive their polite applause and leave the stage, I check my program again to see that Myers is up next. It's a duet: the Handel-Halvorsen Passacaglia for violin and viola—and none other than Hannah McIntyre on the viola.

After their introduction, the two of them take their places on the stage, Hannah carefully placing her score on the music stand. They stand, whereas in the quartets, the performers are seated in deference to the cellists. Myers places his music on his own stand at the last minute and focuses his concentration on the page in front of him. There is a subtle emotion emanating from him that only I can discern, but it is there—indifference, arrogance? Myers is definitely aloof to his partner, something I don't usually see when he takes the stage with someone. They begin. The melodies run pleasingly back and forth, over and under each other, and at times in harmony together. It is in these harmonious renderings of the score that Myers looks up unmistakably from the music, burrowing his glare into Hannah McIntyre. It is so distracting—his obvious disengagement from the page, and his total absorption into her face. Poor, flush-faced Hannah is struggling to focus on the music, and somehow, she keeps up with Myers brilliantly as he seems to pull it out of her with his eyes. It is as if she is under his spell. She concentrates on the music in front of her, but he is glued to her, not the score, and as the duet gathers itself into a fevered pitch, I notice from another fleeting glance at my audience cohorts that they are as spellbound as I am. They are mesmerized at this performance; it is *sexual* at the very least, I think, feeling the heat rise to my own face. I feel Maggie glance my way and I return her look with a wide-eyed response.

I throw my eyes back to the two of them on stage and watch as my son attempts to destroy this young woman, now devoid of any composure she had upon taking the stage just moments ago. I squeeze my eyes shut, and without the visual effect of Hannah's red face, I realize she is somehow managing to play flawlessly under my son's intense scrutiny. The last frenzied measures are upon us, and then the ending has arrived, with Myers swiping his bow across the strings as a final slap in her face. A slap across that lovely cheek for making a fool of him last year, letting her know she wasn't worth the humiliation and doubt he let himself feel. He has made it crystal clear that he has risen above whatever she thought she accomplished by passing over him for another. She will never forget this performance, this afternoon, or this young man who has just tossed her aside, the same way I cast aside his father—eleven years ago.

The audience is stunned momentarily, but then a thunder of applause begins as people spring to their feet in ovation for the tremendous performance they've just witnessed. Surely, there will be talk of this spectacle over dinners and during car rides back home. What was all that about? That slap in the face, that *take that* moment that was obvious to anyone in the room with a pulse! Oh, my God! What am I going to say to Myers? What is he going to say to Hannah? As if words from here on out would have any point! Desecration is the only word I can think of. And *red*—her red face after he'd had his way with her on stage. This showdown has apparently been planned for a long time. Oh, my son, who under normal circumstances would be considered such an introvert, *what have you done to this poor girl?* Did she really deserve all that? I should talk to him about his behavior. He was way over the line. Was I imagining it?

Maggie answers my question in one word.

"Whoa!" she whispers to me from behind her program. "What was *that* all about?"

"Well…" I murmur from the safety of my own booklet in that expansive, Southern one-syllable preamble to something profound. But that is all I have. I have to whisper back since it is oddly quiet in the auditorium even as the students transition for the next piece, another quartet. "I think only Myers can answer that question, but I have a pretty good idea *that* was for last summer's diss."

"Yeah. That's what I thought. Poor Hannah."

So what do you think of this, my love? I ask Stan inwardly, but I get no response. Apparently, stunned like the rest of us, his presence has evaporated into thin air.

It is a quiet ride home for Maggie, Myers, and me. Casey, however, seems as effervescent as ever, possibly charged by Myers's display of testosterone on stage. She, too, falls silent, though, as we cross the state line, and for the next thirty minutes, she keeps her thoughts to herself.

As soon as we are alone in Myers's bedroom, dealing with unpacking his belongings, I have to bring up the incident.

"What was that all about on stage with Hannah?"

Myers contemplates several pairs of boxer shorts as he tosses each one into the dirty clothes pile he's started on his bedroom floor. "Nothing. I was just seeing whether she could keep up with me; that's all."

I don't buy it, but I don't think it's worth the confrontation. Still, an admonition is in order. "Well, whatever it was, you were extremely rude. It didn't go over well, at least with Maggie and me. No telling what Barb Linden thought."

"I'm sorry," he says, looking me straight in the eye. He's learned that the best way to diffuse my attack is to give in immediately and sincerely. It's what I do to his father and it infuriates Kent to no end.

I smirk and take a seat on the end of his bed.

"So did you meet anyone else there who interested you?"

"Yeah, actually, I did. A couple of kids from Asheville were there who are really into playing Celtic music."

"I meant girls."

"I know. And one of the kids is a girl, Sarah Blake." Bingo. I remember her name from the program, the skinny intelligent girl with the veil of light brown hair. I knew it! "But what's the point of starting a new relationship when I'm just going to leave for college at the end of the summer? Still, I might try to get up to Asheville before school starts and check out the music, if you don't mind."

"I think that would be great." I'm dying to know whether he's tried out his condoms, but I know that subject won't be broached. He seems more reserved than usual, but I don't know why. Is it Sarah? Is he embarrassed about what he did to Hannah? Are he and Casey on the outs? He said next to nothing to her in the car. I guess he is ready to be on his own after all. Or maybe he doesn't want me peeking into his suitcase! He looks at me as if I'm suddenly invading his privacy. His voice could be getting tired, or he's just being a boy and he's done talking to me. Trying to read Myers's mind has never been my strong suit. After a moment or two of silently watching him unpack, I decide to leave him alone so I get up off the bed and start to leave his room.

"Mom?"

"What, honey?"

"Did you have fun while I was gone?"

"Yeah. I mean, I didn't do much other than work, but yeah, it was all right." The list. I should tell him something I did off the list so he won't worry. "You know—Pilates and running. I had dinner with Maggie and Barb. It rained a lot so no sailing lessons yet..."

He smiles. "Got it."

And no, I never got around to cleaning out Stan's closet. The rain was depressing enough.

Chapter 8

....

CASEY

....

On Tuesday, we are fortunate enough to catch a break in the weather. The sun came out in the morning, and has stayed out all day, so my patients tell me. I can't wait to get outside and see for myself. Craving the sunshine and two disturbing phone calls have left me unusually distracted today. Yesterday, I picked up my parents from the airport, both sick as dogs, and I left them with a pot of chicken soup from my next favorite restaurant, Almost Home. I called last night to check on them and Mom forbade me to come within a hundred feet of them, assuring me that they will recover. At their age, though, I worry about them. Then, Maggie called last night to let me know we are on this afternoon for our photo shoot. That was only part of the conversation. She'd asked whether Myers or I had heard from Casey. Apparently, the girl had gone AWOL and Maggie was in a dither. Ed was out of town at a visiting-artist-in-residence program, and it seems that trouble always comes to visit when he is gone on one of these junkets. With Meghan, Casey's older sister, away at summer school, and Callum, her older brother at the beach, Maggie was feeling a bit abandoned. I tried to comfort her, reassuring her that she wasn't overreacting. It isn't like Casey to stay out of pocket this way, and I'm sure I'd be freaking out if Myers disappeared like that. It wasn't long ago that Casey had a lapse in judgment and found herself on the wrong end of the law, but I thought she had surely learned her lesson.

"What's the trouble, Dr. Brody? You look like you got a lot on your mind today," Lisa, my office manager, says as we are getting ready to close for the day.

"I'm just thinking about a personal thing, Lisa. My friend hasn't heard from her daughter; at least, I don't know if she has.... I meant to call her today and check on her, but we were so slammed I didn't get a chance."

"You got that right. Did you even eat your lunch today?"

"No, come to think of it, I didn't. Did you?"

"No, ma'am. My stomach's been growling all afternoon."

"Well, go home. Enjoy the sunshine—and your dinner!"

"Thanks, you too! You got a date tonight? You're all dressed up."

She is referring to the black dress I'm wearing again. I suppose I do look dressed up, but of course, I am not wearing the red shoes. I'd never hear the end of that! It appears that everyone is on my love-life watch.

"No, just...." I shrug distractedly, not knowing how to respond.

⟡

On the way to Maggie's, I use my cell phone to check in with Mom, who sounds terrible, making me swear to stay away at all costs. When I arrive at Maggie's house, there is no sign of Casey's presence. I carry in my tote bag with the red shoes to find Maggie on the phone with her mother. She motions me inside and points out the broomstick on the dining room table beside her camera. It is blessedly cool inside; I am aware that my hair has curled another inch shorter just from the ride over in the late afternoon heat and humidity. Holding up a finger, she goes back into her kitchen to talk to her mother, while I rest my purse on her sofa and consider putting on the shoes. Judging by the look on her face, I'm not sure we're still doing our shoot, but at least she can check out the shoes and the outfit, complete with the broom, for effect. I hope her client isn't in any big hurry for this book cover.

I slip out of my black pumps and reach into the bag for the red shoes. It takes a bit of doing to tug them on and then some balance readjustment when I stand up in them. I know this is what she has in mind, but good grief! How do women seriously walk in these things? I make my way over to the dining room table and reach for my broomstick prop as I hear her trying to wrap up her conversation with her mom. There is a lot to explain and her mother's worry to abate as she deals with her own. Then I hear Maggie mention something about the police and a bad feeling takes over immediately. At the same time, I catch a glimpse of myself in her dining room mirror, but I can't see my feet. Something about the broomstick makes me decide to pose while I'm waiting for her, and I laugh in spite of myself. What a picture! But maybe this could work, I think, rearranging my hair in the mirror. I need to soften my lips, so I go to my purse and look for lip gloss—*Very Berry*. Much better.

Before she returns, I hear footsteps on the front porch along with the doorbell.

"Oh, shit!" I mutter under my breath. Could this be the police? And here I stand, looking like I'm expecting Glinda, the Good Witch of the North! I teeter back into the dining room and put the broomstick back on the table as quickly as I can. There are definitely two men at the door, and one is a police officer. Crap! I should take off these ridiculous shoes, but then, wouldn't it seem worse to greet them in my bare feet? There isn't time to wonder, with Maggie still wrapped up with her mom, so I go to the door, open it, and try not to gasp.

Detective Chase and the officer stand a safe distance from the door, the way repairmen do so people won't be alarmed when they fling open the door to find strangers waiting. Chase is wearing a gray suit and looking hot—sweating, actually. The previous week's worth of rain has left a great deal of South Carolina humidity in its wake.

"Oh! Hello, Detective Chase!" We exchange surprised looks, complete with both sets of our eyebrows raised in shock. I feel the instant flush of heat rise to my cheeks as my presence registers on his face.

"Uh, hi—I was expecting Mrs. French. How are you, Dr. Brody?"

"I—oh, Susannah, please—Maggie's on the phone with her mother. Won't you come in?"

He's staring at my red shoes. Of course he is. There couldn't be a more distracting spectacle, and I am not at all what he was expecting. I wasn't expecting him either!

"I—I'm—sorry!" I stammer, straightening first my dress and then my hair, but neither of those is the problem. His investigative eyes are glued to my legs.

He clears his throat. "No—it's fine, I mean, you look...*lethal*," he finally gets out matter-of-factly. I'd forgotten that he has a slow, southern drawl. I would guess he's from Alabama or Georgia, but I could be wrong. I have a vague recollection of a conversation with Patti about where he was from.

I wave my hand as if it's no big deal that I'm dressed this way. "We were supposed to do a photoshoot today, but that's probably not happening. I take it Casey is still missing?"

He looks confused, as though I should know, since I'm standing in Maggie's foyer in my Halloween costume. He nods and gestures to his colleague.

"This is Officer Roberts."

"Hi. Please, come in. I think I hear her wrapping it up. Can I get either of you a glass of water?"

I can at least play hostess, and water is one thing I can manage while my head swims.

"Yes, thank you. That would be great. Want some water, Roberts?" Chase steps inside, into the coolness of the house gratefully, inserting a finger under his collar and looking around for Maggie, who is finally emerging from the kitchen with her cell phone in hand. The officer looks as if he is melting as well, and he graciously accepts the water offer.

"Hello! Detective Chase? Hi, I'm Maggie French," she says, extending her hand to shake his, while catching a glimpse of me in full regalia. "Oh, wow! That looks so great! I'm sorry I didn't get to tell you," she says to me, shooting a look back at Chase. "I guess you figured out that Casey is still missing."

"Yes! I'm so sorry," I say, leaning down to give her a hug. I'm towering over my friend, but I'm right at eye level with Chase. I can smell him perspiring, and I get a whiff of sunscreen, mixed with his subtle cologne. It's an altogether pleasant sensation. *Good for you, Chase.* I find myself examining his face for further lesions I should attend to. It's an annoying occupational hazard I can't seem to shake. I try to focus on my friend. "I wanted to call you today, but I was slammed all day at the office. I was just going to get a glass of water for Officer Roberts and Detective Chase—would you like one?"

"Actually, something stronger would be my preference, but I guess that can wait."

I take my cue to go for the water while Maggie ushers the men into the living room and I hear them taking seats and the sound of paper rustling and a pen clicking. Chase is getting down to business.

"Officer Roberts will be collecting fingerprints while we talk. We'll need to get your prints as well, and anyone else's who's living in the house...."

"I'm the only one in the house who's home. That doesn't sound right, does it?" she laughs nervously. "I meant, my husband's away on business, and my other children are—well, one is at the beach for the summer and the other is at summer school at USC," Maggie explains.

"Oh, both of my kids go there," he says in an easy voice, just like any other person you'd meet, helping Maggie relax.

"How many children do you have?" she asks as I return with his water. He accepts it gratefully, thanking me and eyeing the shoes again. I'm trying my best not to topple over and appear as if I dress this way on a daily basis. Officer Roberts accepts his glass and goes on about his business. His presence is sobering.

"I have two—a boy and a girl. Ryan will be a senior next year and Olivia will be a sophomore," he says pleasantly, but it's apparent he is ready to get started with his investigation. He takes a sip of his water.

"So when was the last time you saw Casey, Mrs. French?"

"Please call me Maggie. She was here Monday morning—yesterday— when I left for work. I work at Dream Weavers Art Gallery part-time, and—well, the rest of the time, I work from home. I'm a graphic designer. Anyway," she says, putting her fingertips to her head, trying to get the details straight for Chase. "I left around eight-thirty and she was still asleep. When I got back home at three o'clock, she was gone. I thought she'd walked up to the pool. Her car is still here…" She clears her throat and pauses, which allows us to see the tears welling up in her eyes. "It's very uncharacteristic of Casey to disappear like this."

I move to sit beside her on the sofa, where I can take her hand in mine. Chase watches and turns his endless green eyes back on Maggie.

"Let's get some statistics first. Do you know Casey's height and weight? I also need her hair color," he says calmly, writing notes on his pad—*8:30 home, 3:00 gone, car here.* I look away when he notices my intrusive eyes on his notepad. He doubts everything, believes nothing.

"She's five-one and she weighs 130, maybe 140 pounds...do you agree, Susannah?"

I shrug, then nod. I hate trying to guess people's weight. It doesn't seem politically correct.

"Her hair is sort of a dirty blond, down to here," Maggie says, indicating the area right above her shoulder. Chase is writing it all down.

"Date of birth?"

"April 15, 1995."

"Tax day. Has Casey ever disappeared before?"

"No."

"Are you missing a suitcase she might have used?"

"Yes. I even checked the trunk of both of our cars, and it's gone. It was the one she took to camp."

He nods and I imagine he's thinking Casey left of her own will. It appears that way to me, but then he squints very slightly at Maggie, re-evaluating the situation, perhaps. *What is he thinking now?*

"Who all have you contacted to check on her whereabouts, Maggie?"

"I called Susannah first, to see if Myers had been with her or heard from her at all. Myers is her son, and Casey's best friend. They've just come home from a two-week music camp at the North Carolina School of the Arts." Chase makes notes and then waits for her to continue. "I called her brother and sister, her dad, of course, to let him know what's happening, and then I've called her girlfriends, Kristen and Kelsey. They're girls from school she does things with occasionally. They haven't seen Casey all summer—which is what I thought, but you know...."

"Of course. Did she make any new friends at the music camp?"

"I'm sure she did. Casey's never met a stranger. She mentioned a boy named Daniel Yoo. He was in one of her quartets, but that was the extent of it."

"Do you know where Daniel lives?" he asks, writing down the name.

"No, I'm afraid we didn't get that far."

As Chase gazes at Maggie for a moment, I feel the need to close my mouth. Those eyes of his are fathomless. He seems so nice when he asks the next question, but I know he's wondering what else could be amiss in this household.

"Has Casey been upset about anything recently? Angry with you and her father, maybe?"

Maggie glances at me and rubs the back of her neck. "No. Not really."

"Has she seemed unusually depressed? Not herself?"

"No."

"Has she mentioned anyone else being upset with her? A quarrel with a friend? Anyone calling her and annoying her?"

"No."

"Does she have any health issues we should know about?"

"No."

"Has she mentioned wanting to hurt herself?"

"Oh, no, nothing like that," Maggie says, shaking off the image.

"Did she have a job over the summer?"

"No. She's been too busy with all her theater and musical events."

Chase probes her with his eyes, and he checks me at the same time briefly. "Tell me about that." He seems so professional and all business. I try to imagine him sitting on the couch with Patti, watching TV and eating popcorn....

He writes as Maggie relates Casey's musical talent and her recent foray into the theater. She gives a ghost of an eye roll, making Chase cock his head slightly.

"Is there a problem with the plays?"

Maggie shrugs. "Oh, well, her father and I have been trying to dissuade Casey from her interest in the theater. She's much more talented as a musician, and we'd love for her to pursue a piano performance major or cello, but acting is not something we think she should pursue."

"Why not?" he asks.

"Well...theater people are a dime a dozen and she is so new at it. She doesn't really have...the looks for theater, which will limit her to character roles, which she seems okay with, but she could be outstanding in the musical pursuits. Then there's the issue of going to USC...." Maggie says.

"What's the issue?"

"Casey isn't too excited to be going there."

"Why not? It's a great school," Chase says.

"Well...I know it is. My other daughter goes there as well, but Casey had a scholarship to the Juilliard School until she had a little brush with the law. Her scholarship was revoked and Ed and I are tight on finances with all three of them in college, so Casey is going to have to attend USC in the fall, and she's really not very excited about it."

"Oh. I see," he says and writes down the details. "I saw in her records that she was convicted of a misdemeanor drug charge last January?"

"Yes, she got busted for smoking pot back in the winter with a boy from school. She's been to court and has finished out her community service requirements, attended her drug and alcohol classes, and gone to counseling. The judge will expunge her record when all the paperwork is completed, but the whole experience has been somewhat altering for her, for all of us. More than just a bump in the road."

"And the boy who was charged with her, Spencer Wilson?" Chase asks, flipping back a page or two in his notes.

"Yes. He's a boy she met in the drama club at school, but they severed their ties right after all this happened."

99

"Are you sure?"

"I think so. She doesn't talk about him, and I haven't been aware that they've been in contact."

"Have you contacted Spencer since Casey went missing?"

"No."

"Does Casey have a cell phone or a laptop or a tablet?" Chase asks brusquely.

"Yes, she has a phone and a laptop, but both of those are missing as well."

"Is she on your cell phone plan? If she is, you can look over the phone records and see who she's been contacting. Does she access Facebook that you know of?"

"Yes."

"And do you happen to know her password?"

"No."

"Does she ever browse the Internet from another computer in this house?"

"Not in some time. She usually gets on her laptop and we don't see her for hours."

Chase smiles for the first time, making both of us relax. "I know how that is!"

He gives Maggie a long glance and takes a deep breath. "Do you have a recent picture of Casey?" When she nods, he continues. "I'd also like to get a warrant for your phone records, bank accounts, social media, maybe a handwriting sample. But that probably won't happen until to-morrow...and we'd only ask for DNA if we conclude there is reasonable cause to need it. DNA testing takes time and it's expensive. I need to take a look around."

"Oh, of course. Here's her picture," Maggie says, eyes wide at the mention of DNA, going to the mantle and removing a framed photo of Casey's senior picture. *DNA is serious.* She leads Chase upstairs to Casey's room and I teeter along behind them, holding a hand out to Maggie's back. She is so pale and shaky that I'm afraid she'll keel over at any moment. Officer Roberts follows us and begins dusting items in Casey's room for prints and glances at Chase. Chase walks over to Casey's desk and looks over the memorabilia, books, and papers, much like what is all over Myers's desk at my house.

Chase looks over the paperwork on the desk. He seems to want to look through the envelopes but refrains. Maggie explains that the large envelopes on Casey's desk are college correspondence, while Chase turns his attention to me.

"Uh, Susannah, I'd like to talk to your son as well. He might be able to shed some more light on the situation. Maybe he knows something."

"Sure. They were at the same music camp for the last two weeks. He might know some of the kids she met there."

"That's what I'm hoping. Where has he been over the last two days?"

My mouth goes dry, and his pointed question gives me an idea of what Maggie has been feeling for the last several minutes.

"Uh...he's been at home as far as I know. He hasn't felt very well and he slept most of yesterday. I came straight here from work. I called him but didn't get an answer. That's not highly unusual though," I add.

Chase makes me feel better. "That's typical of my two as well," he says, giving me that cute grin again.

"Here's some of her college paperwork," Maggie says, showing Chase a booklet she's found in one of the envelopes. "This is her school ID number and here's her password."

"*CF88keys!...*" he says, frowning, and writing it down on his pad.

"The piano keyboard has eighty-eight keys," she explains.

"Oh. Smart. And easy to remember and type. Probably her Facebook password, too," he murmurs. *He's giving Maggie ideas*, I think to myself. He wouldn't if he suspected she's had anything to do with Casey's disappearance.

Chase makes a sweep of Casey's bathroom, looking into an empty wastebasket and looking over the shower tub. We go back downstairs and I reach into my purse for my own cell phone.

"Would it be better for Myers to come over here?" I ask Chase, thinking that this could take forever. Maggie sits at the dining room table, opens her laptop, and starts typing.

"If you can reach him, that'd be great."

I feel a mild degree of panic creep inside my chest as I press the place on my phone screen that should connect me to my son. *What if he's gone too?* It's not a good feeling, I think, as I listen to the second ring and thankfully Myers's voice answers, "Hey, Mom."

"Oh, thank God! I called about an hour ago and you didn't answer."

"I was in the shower. Tim and I got back from the pool about then. Where are you?"

"I'm over here at Maggie's. Casey is still missing. Detective Chase is here and would like to have a word with you. Can you come over?"

Chase ignores me, or so it appears, as he watches Maggie. She's looking on Facebook, and I wonder whether she has thought about snooping into Casey's account. I guess parents do it all the time, but it seems weird, an invasion of her privacy, and nothing I would ever do to Myers. But should I? Maggie has logged into Facebook and is showing Casey's page to Chase. She can't see Casey's messages, but she has accessed a list of Casey's friends, and my son's face pops up immediately. As Chase scratches his face, I notice the glint of his wedding band. He still wears his, too. We have something in common.

"Yeah, okay. I'll drop Tim off on the way. I can be there in three minutes," Myers says.

"Okay. Thank you."

Three minutes. The joys of a small town. We won't have to keep Detective Chase waiting long, and maybe we can get to the bottom of Casey's disappearance.

Chase looks up from the screen. "Casey is eighteen, correct?"

"Yes. She turned eighteen in April."

"Myers?"

"He turned eighteen at the beginning of June."

"Well, it does appear they are close," Chase says, a smile starting at some of the pictures he's seeing with Myers and Casey clowning around on the screen. "Was Myers upset that she was missing?" Chase's question catches me off-guard.

"Oh—well, with Myers, it's hard to tell sometimes. He seemed concerned, but it also seemed like he thought we were overreacting."

"How so?" Those eyes are searing into me. Does he think I'm lying? I'm trying to be as honest as possible.

"Well... the parents I was just talking to at the music camp are all saying how annoyed their children are with them right now. With all of our kids preparing to head off for college in a few weeks, they seem to get really tired of us keeping tabs on them. Myers is no exception," I say with a smile, wishing Chase would lighten up. He does. He smiles at me again.

"It's hard letting go," he says thoughtfully.

What? I've heard that before, disturbingly recently, too. Chase turns to Maggie while I daydream about Stan momentarily.

"Maggie, does Casey have a bank account?"

"Yes, we set up a checking account for her last summer when she worked in the concession stand up at the pool."

"Do you have access to her account online?" he asks, looking at her computer.

"Sure," Maggie says, fingering the keys and tapping in her bank's website. In a moment, she has accessed the account and we hear her gasp. "Oh! Look at this. She had over $1500 and now there's only $200 and something in the account. She withdrew $1300 yesterday."

Chills run down my arms. My stomach growls, but no one notices.

"Do you think she withdrew it of her own will, or could someone have forced her to do it?" Maggie asks and Detective Chase shrugs.

"Either of these is a possibility, but regardless, it looks like she was planning to leave town—with that much cash in hand."

Maggie and I exchange a glance. Officer Roberts is back downstairs, waiting to take Maggie's fingerprints.

Chase says kindly, "Maggie, there doesn't seem to be evidence of any struggle or wrongdoing here. You do need to be aware that if there is no foul play in evidence, with Casey's being eighteen, it's within her rights to leave home of her own accord. And if that's the case here, then there's really nothing more the police department can do. But, still, I have a feeling something's not right, and until we know for sure that she's safe, we'll look into all the possibilities."

Maggie sags in her chair at the dining room table. "Thank you. I mean, I hope that's all it is. Maybe she'll call me and tell me where she is. Maybe she'll come walking back in here and tell me she tried to get in touch with me...or something," she says, and then her face crumbles. She covers her face with both hands.

"Oh, God! This is so weird! I keep thinking I can just walk into a room and she'll be there, but she's not." Chase and I exchange glances. We both know that feeling all too well. "It's like a nightmare! I don't know what to think. What if she *has* been abducted somehow…or hurt, and I don't know where she is? Susannah? Could she have run off with some *guy?* I just don't *know!* I *hate* this! I hate not knowing and I hate that Ed's not here.…"

It is at that moment that Myers opens the front door and walks in, as if he lives here.

"Have you talked to Ed about coming home?" I ask Maggie as we stand up to introduce Myers to Detective Chase.

"He's on standby. I'll call him in a little while. I think he needs to get here right now. Hey, Myers!" Maggie says, giving my son a hug, and he gives her a big one in return.

"Hey, Maggie. I'm sorry about Casey."

"Oh…thanks, honey," she says, letting him go.

"Myers, this is Detective Chase from the Fort Mill Police Department," I say to him, gesturing to Chase. "This is my son—Myers Morgan."

"Hey, Myers," Chase says, shaking Myers's hand and giving him that unnerving stare. Myers swallows.

"Hey," Myers says, meeting the gaze with his own steady one. "Any news about Casey?"

"Nothing yet. I'd like to ask you some questions if I may."

"Sure," says Myers, and Chase gestures that they sit at the table while Maggie goes with Officer Roberts, who asks her to follow him into the kitchen to take her fingerprints.

"So, Myers, when was the last time you saw Casey?"

"Uh, I guess Saturday, when we all came back from Winston-Salem."

"When was the last time you talked to her?"

"Same day."

"You didn't talk to her on the phone?"

"No."

"How about on Facebook?"

"No."

Chase looks at Myers with that deep intensity, making me wonder whether he's uncovered something and is now trying to catch Myers in a lie.

"Any idea where she might be?"

"Like I told Mom, no idea."

"So, you guys were at music camp together?"

"Yeah."

"What do you play?"

"Violin."

"Classical?"

"Yeah—and blues, Celtic, bluegrass, and country. I play it all, but country's my favorite."

Chase seems duly impressed. "What are your plans for the fall, Myers?"

"I'll be going to Belmont University," Myers says, keeping up with Chase's light line of questioning. Our detective cocks his head.

"I don't know it. Where is Belmont?"

"Nashville. Belmont has an excellent music department. Nashville's where I wanna stay and work when I'm done."

"Oh. Great plan. Did you and Casey meet some people at the camp?"

"Yeah, a few."

"Who did she meet that you think she might keep up with?"

"Well, there was Daniel Yoo…and Sarah Blake and Michael Moline."

Chase asks him to write down their names.

"I'd like your cell phone numbers too, both of you, please," he says, offering the pad to me. Then he turns back to Myers.

"Myers, if you were Casey and wanted to get away somewhere special, where would you go?"

Myers meets his dead-on gaze without blinking.

"Nowhere. I'd stay right here. Tahiti maybe...."

Chase studies him a moment. I glance at Myers, one of my eyebrows raised in warning. *Now is no time to be a smart-aleck.* I write down my contact information as Myers sits silently at the table. Maggie is back from the kitchen with Officer Roberts, wiping the fingerprinting ink off her fingers.

"Well, I think we're all done here for the moment," Chase says. "I'll get started checking with the public transportation systems to see whether Casey might have taken a taxi, a bus, or a train, or maybe even hopped a plane somewhere. I'll request warrants for Casey's social media accounts, phone records, and your bank accounts. You'll all let me know if something else comes to you, okay? And of course, if she or someone else contacts any of you, call me ASAP," he says, handing each of us a card. We take the cards and Chase stands, collecting his briefcase. I hand him the pad and he studies our contact information, and then he slips it in the briefcase, zipping it soundly.

"Thanks, Detective Chase...Officer," Maggie says as she and I walk them to the door.

Chase glances at each of us; then he gives my legs one last, long appraising look and says, "I'll be in touch tomorrow, or if anything pops before then. Have a good evening."

Chapter 9

OFF BALANCE

Maggie and I watch Chase through her front door window as he strides down her walkway to his car. On any other day I know she'd say, *that is one attractive man,* in that tone that tells me I should be thinking the same thing, but she is too distraught to bring it up. Myers, on the other hand, seems completely unfazed as he gawks openly at my outfit.

"Mom. What are you wearing?"

"Oh, I'm Maggie's model for a book cover shoot and she wanted me to wear this. She and I, uh, you know, had a photoshoot planned until I realized that Casey was still missing, and then Detective Chase and the other cop showed up," I say, glad to peel my feet out of the stilettos.

Maggie laughs. "You know, we'd probably better go ahead and do that shoot before the weather messes us up again."

"But don't you want to stay here in case you hear from Casey?"

Maggie shrugs, extending her hands helplessly. "Well, I've thought about this all day. If she's left of her own volition, there isn't much I can do about it, and sitting here all day isn't going to bring her home."

"Really?"

"Yeah, I'm okay with it. Besides, doing the shoot will get my mind off of her for a little while. I'm glad to have a diversion, actually. And I have my cell phone in case anybody calls, so it doesn't really matter where I am."

My stomach growls again as I give her a chin-up kind of smile.

"Why don't we eat some dinner? I'm starving! I've been marinating some chicken and I have peppers, and I was thinking about making fajitas tonight. Does that sound good? Will you stay, Myers?" she asks, going into her kitchen as we follow like baby ducks behind her. The woman is never still.

"Sure," says Myers with a shrug.

"Here, I made sangria, Susannah," she says, her head lost in the refrigerator. "I have some tea, Myers, and some lemonade. Want a half-and-half?"

"Sure," he says again while she produces three pitchers from the fridge.

"What can I do?" I ask as she's apparently masking her distress in a feeding frenzy. She sets green, yellow, and red bell peppers on her kitchen island and hands me an onion.

"If you'll chop these, I'll get out the chicken and then I'll pour our drinks! And then after we eat, we can go and take some pictures. It shouldn't take more than an hour, and by then the lighting will be better anyway."

Myers and I watch her carefully, as if she is an escaped inmate from a mental ward. When she turns her back to look for glasses in the cupboard, he catches my eye and raises his eyebrows.

"Okay," I tell her. "Maybe Myers can hold down the fort in case Casey wanders back in while we're gone," I suggest and he nods. He looks concerned, and I have questions, but I don't ask while Maggie is attempting to move on.

"That would be great," she says, winking at my son. I know she and Myers have already talked about Casey, so I need to let it go. *It's time to let go.*

I don't want to let go. I don't want to let go of *anyone.* Is this one more instance in which we've lost a loved one when we could have prevented it? If we'd just known what was bothering Casey, maybe we could have kept her from leaving? I know she's left. There's nothing to indicate that she was kidnapped or hurt in a home invasion or anything that mothers have nightmares about when they should be sleeping soundly. My imagination spirals out of control as I chop the multi-colored peppers into slender strips. I wonder what Myers is thinking as he drinks his half-and-half and Maggie instructs him to open a can of black beans and put them in a pot. I wonder what is going through Maggie's mind. Could she have kept Casey at home? What in the world went wrong? All of us want to help, but we feel so out of control.

I could have helped Patti Chase. I could have helped Stan, too if I'd known his medical history, if any of us had known. I sigh, wondering why I'm going down this path. That's the trouble with the unwanted; no one knows anything until it's too late. Stan's father left them when he was young. His mother brought him to the States when he was sixteen. He was like me—no known family medical history other than his mother's. But I have none. What lurks in my DNA that I don't know about? *And the police might need something with Casey's DNA on it....* I shudder.

"Susannah?"

"Sorry. What?"

"You like cilantro, right?"

"Oh, yes. I love it."

"Great. I'll go clip us some out of my garden for the fajitas. And while I'm out there, I'm going to call Ed to update him and make him come home right now."

When she has slipped out her back door with her cell phone, I glance at Myers. "You really have no idea where Casey is?" I can't help but ask.

He gives me an irritated look while he rinses out the black bean can and tosses it under her sink, in the recycle bin. We could both live here; we are so familiar with Maggie's habits. I munch on a slice of the yellow pepper.

"Mom. Don't start. You sound like Detective Chase."

"Have you tried her cell?" He glares at me so I explain my thinking. "I just—can't imagine where Casey would go and not tell Maggie…or *you*. It's not like her."

"And smoking weed with Spencer Wilson wasn't *like her*?"

He's still upset about that. She'd taken a break from Myers to hang out with her drama friend, Spencer, and look what it cost her. "Myers. That's in the past. I want to think Casey has grown up."

"We both have." He's touchy. Maybe she's leaving him out again.

"I know. You are so responsible. And I thought she was too."

The door whooshes open and Maggie is back. "Oh, it is so humid out there! Hopefully, when we go to take our pictures, it will be a little bit better. Ed is on his way home."

She takes my bowl of sliced peppers and mixes them in with her marinated chicken as I sip my sangria. It's delicious and refreshing, and she picks up her glass to sip her own. Myers and I watch as she rinses the cilantro, blots it dry with a paper towel, and proceeds to chop it on my cutting board. She sips her drink again, thinks a minute, and then looks at us.

"I've racked my brain and can't understand what's happened to my girl. Do you think Casey has taken a lover we don't know about?"

❦

At lunch the following day, I check in with Maggie. Surely there is news and I am right in believing that Casey has taken herself off on some kind of joyride.

"You won't believe what I found, Suz! I was taking a coffee filter out of the cabinet to put it into the coffeemaker, and there was a note on it from Casey! She knew I would pull one out this morning and see it today."

The blueberry yogurt stops halfway to my mouth as I gasp.

"What did it say?"

"It says, *'Mama, don't worry about me. I'm trying something out and I'll call you next week. I'm fine, but don't try to find me. You'd just make me come home. Love, Casey.'* Can you believe that?"

I can't tell whether Maggie is angry or relieved. "What do you think?" I ask her.

"I think she's trying out those *condoms* is what I think! I'm *so pissed!* I'm relieved, too. And so embarrassed! I have a call in to Detective Chase. Oh, and I did a little sleuthing myself last night. I went through her college paperwork and used that password I found to access her Facebook account *and bingo.* That was her password."

"Oh, boy! What'd you find?" Detective Chase certainly led her down that handy little path. *Oh, look what else I found....*

"Okay, tell me how an eighteen-year-old girl from Magnolia Village has 943 friends? I spent hours going through all her contacts and messages. There's nothing in there to indicate that she ran off with somebody. What is Chase going to think about us now?"

"Oh, don't worry about him. I'm sure he'll take it all in stride. Don't you know, he's seen it all?"

"Well, you're probably right, but I'll tell you what—Ed French is madder than a wet hen! He stumbled in from Asheville last night at midnight, and it looks like he's going right back up there today...when he stops yelling, that is! I've never seen him so angry. It's scary!"

"He's fighting for control." Ed French is the most controlling man I've ever met, and having his daughter rebel like this on several occasions has almost done the poor man in!

"I know! I find myself trying to defend her. What's wrong with me?"

"You just want to think she's doing something reasonable, when in fact it doesn't seem reasonable at all. I'm glad she's okay. Or at least, we think she's okay."

"Oh, I hope she hasn't gone off with some psychopath who's sucked her into his sick game. I wonder if she was on one of those dating websites? Or what if she's gone off with another *girl?* I was up half the night worrying that she's decided she's *gay* and can't tell me."

"Okay, now you've gone off the deep end. Want me to come over after I leave the office?"

"Do you mind?"

"Not at all. I'll bring dinner. I have to check on Mom and Dad first. I'll take them something too."

"What's Myers doing tonight? He can come too. I like having him around."

"I think he's going to open mike night at the Limerick Café with Tim. I'm sure he can fend for himself for dinner. I'll call him and make sure, so count on me as soon as I can get away, okay?"

"Thanks. You're such a good friend! And you can see the book cover when you get here. In my sleepless state last night, I worked on it. I sent it to the client at three this morning and she loves it!"

"You need to sleep, Maggie. Can you take a nap this afternoon?"

"I won't be able to rest."

"I'll bring you some melatonin so you can crash tonight."

"I've never tried it."

"It works. I've been taking it before bed since Stan died."

There is a brief hesitation before she says, "Okay, I'll try it. I'll see you later."

I stop in again at Almost Home to purchase three chicken pies. Cheryl, the owner, is used to seeing me at least three times a week. I like to cook, but I often don't have the energy at the end of a busy day. I thank her and leave with my parcel, driving to my parents' house first. My mother appears at the door, looking paler than usual, but at least she is up and moving. I am relieved to see her, given all the drama in our lives these days. She recoils when I throw my arms around her.

"Oh, darling, don't hug me! You'll catch your death!" Her sandy hair is cut short and her bangs fringe her face, making her look like a pixie, and in this heat, she wears a pale green housecoat that sets off her eyes in a pleasing way. However ill she is feeling, she seems delighted to see me, and I return the look.

"Mom! How are you? Any better?"

"Somewhat, dear," she says, covering her mouth out of respect for my health.

"How's Dad?"

"He's getting better. He's actually taking a shower, which is more than I've done. Did you bring us dinner?"

"I did. Cheryl's chicken pie from Almost Home."

"Oh, my favorite!" she says, following me into her kitchen where I place their container on the stove top. "How is Myers?"

"He's doing all right. You know, Casey French has been missing for a couple of days now, and I think we're all just a bit out of sorts."

"I know; your dad told me after you'd checked in on us last night. Still no word?"

"We think she left and went somewhere. She left a note for Maggie on a coffee filter that Maggie found this morning. Can you imagine? She said not to worry and she'd call in a week."

My mother looks astounded. "Good grief! Why can't she just call and reassure her poor mother that way?"

I shake my head. "I don't know. Something about it isn't right. We don't know what she's up to."

My mother slides onto a barstool at the kitchen counter and rests her arms on it to support herself. "I'd wring her little neck."

"So would I! And so would Maggie. Maggie thinks she's gone after a guy, but we really don't know anything."

"Your dad said she'd called the police. Are they doing anything?"

"Yes. There's a detective working on the case, and Maggie's been trying to catch up with him all day. I'm on my way over as soon as I drop off a pie for Myers. He and Tim are going to open mike night at the Limerick tonight."

"Oh, such fun. Give him my love. If I felt better, I'd go listen to him myself. I think I need to go collapse now." She grins half-heartedly and walks me to the door.

I look at her. She is the nicest person I know, aside from my dad. "Hey, thanks again for the *Stan the Man* book. I really love it, you know?"

"I'm glad you like it, dear. And here—take these squash home with you. Our neighbor picked them for us from our garden, but I'm in no shape to cook them up."

"Thanks, Myers will love it. Squash is one of his favorites. Bye, Mom. I hope you both feel better. I really want to sit and hear all about your trip."

"Okay. We'll do it soon. Bye, honey. Thanks for the dinner."

I open the door to my own house and set my second chicken pie and my sack of squash on the counter. There is two days' worth of mail in a pile that I choose to ignore for the moment, wondering where Myers is. I can hear him walking around upstairs. His phone rings, but it's not a familiar sound. He must have changed his ringtone at camp. I hear a quiet exchange and then he comes downstairs, padding barefoot into the kitchen.

"Hi, Mom. I thought that was you." He looks so pale.

"Hey! Are you okay? I thought you were feeling better."

"Yeah, I'm just tired. I was sleeping. Aren't you going to Maggie's tonight?" he asks, stretching and yawning.

"I am, but I brought you some dinner before I go over there."

"Oh, okay, thanks," he says, glancing at the pie on the counter. Chicken pie is his favorite too, but he's not exactly "cutting flips," as Jen would say.

"What time will you be home tonight?"

"Uh, I guess around eleven-thirty. Don't wait up, okay?"

"Oh, right," I say, rolling my eyes. "I'll be looking at the clock. You know I never sleep until I know you're in, safe and sound."

"Will you be able to sleep at all when I go to college?"

I laugh. There's finally a glint in his eye.

"Probably not at all the first week. Then I'll be too tired to worry about you."

He shifts his weight to his other foot, as if he's ready for me to go.

"Okay, I'm off. You might want to heat this up before you eat it. Just don't forget to turn off the oven."

"Got it. Tell Maggie I said, 'Hey.'"

"I will. Oh, by the way, she said she got a note from Casey."

"Oh, really? What'd it say?"

I explain and he listens with mild interest. "What does Detective Chase think about it?"

"I don't know. Maggie was waiting to hear from him when we spoke at lunch."

I rise up on my toes to give him a kiss on the cheek and he lets me, not so reluctantly. "Bye, kiddo."

"See you, Mom."

Maggie and I are sitting in the study she uses for her office. We're having another glass of her fine sangria as she scrolls through our photos on her laptop. Her office is a cheery place. She has decorated it with antique white-painted furniture, and there are apple green leather containers that hold her various supplies and projects. A large painting of a field of poppies hangs on the wall behind her, and the other walls are adorned with many of her photographs: nature scenes and portraits of family and friends. A shot of Casey stands out. In it, she is a little girl in pink sequins, singing into a wire whisk. It's always been my favorite. It's so *Casey*.

"I'll show you all the photos in a minute, but here's the book cover. What do you think?" she asks, turning the laptop around so I can see it.

And there I am. The photo is me, standing rigidly with my back to the camera in the black dress and red shoes, holding the broomstick up like an offering, in front of the largest most dramatic, corporate doors there are in the city of Charlotte. Maggie has used special effects, so the scene looks hauntingly surreal. At the top of the photo the words in silver foil text read, *Working for the Wizard, a novel,* and at the bottom, the author's name is printed in silver block letters. For a moment, I am taken in, as if the person in the photograph is someone else. The effect leaves one wondering what the woman has had to do to present the broomstick to the wizard, much like Dorothy's predicament in *The Wizard of Oz*. Overall, I believe Maggie has nailed the concept.

"I love it! I can't believe that's me."

"I know! Aren't you sexy? Look at your legs! They go on for miles! The client loved it, too. I knew she would. She said it was perfect. I'm waiting to see whether they want any changes, but so far, I think we have a hit on our hands."

"Now I want to read the book!" I say, grinning stupidly at my own image on the screen, as the doorbell rings.

"Oh, that's Detective Chase!" she says, collecting her laptop and leading me back into the foyer. I open the door since Maggie is armed with her sangria and the laptop.

"Hi," I greet him, wondering how many other cases he's working if he shows up here at seven every night.

His eyes run up and down my figure, checking my current costume, no doubt, before he speaks. Tonight, I look back to normal in a blouse, slacks, and matching shoes with comfortable wedge heels. This time he is taller than I am, by just an inch.

He doesn't seem surprised to find me here. "Hi, Doctor—Susannah, I mean."

"Come on in," I reply, holding the door for him, and he enters, briefcase in hand, wearing a tan suit tonight with a nice blue shirt and striped tie. He's not sweating this evening.

"Hi, Detective Chase. What's the news?" Maggie asks, leading us to sit at the dining room table where she sets the laptop and opens it, in case she needs to access accounts.

"I was finally able to obtain a court order to review your bank accounts and phone records, as well as any of Casey's social media accounts. I didn't find any online dating accounts under her name, or any other social media accounts other than Facebook."

"Well, I've already perused her Facebook account. I used that password and it got me right in," says Maggie as Chase's eyes glint with a knowing look.

"What did you discover?"

"A lot of overwhelming contacts. I was looking for people I'd never heard of before, thinking she's hooked up with someone new. She has a gazillion 'friends' so it could take years to find anything worth noting. Way more than half of them are people from outside Magnolia Village."

"Huh," he says, neither congratulating her, nor condemning her spying. "I looked through it as well, and you're right; she's a popular young lady. Lots of people want her to 'come and see them.' Well, aside from that, I went around to the train station and bus terminal today and did some checking to see whether she took any rides anywhere. I didn't find her name anywhere on any of the passenger manifests. Nobody from the cab companies in the area picked up anyone in the village on Monday after eight-thirty in the morning. Her name doesn't show up on any of the airlines manifests for that day either."

"Could she be using another name?" I ask.

"Like *Chardonnay French*?" Maggie blurts and we laugh. Chase looks at us, apparently wondering at our inappropriate outburst.

"It's just that my daughter loves to indulge in frequent delusions of grandeur. She's constantly making up stage names for herself!" Maggie says, and he nods.

"Maybe you should check for Nellie Forbush, or Tracy Turnblad," I throw in. He looks confused.

"Those are two of the characters she's played recently—the leading female roles in *South Pacific* and *Hairspray*."

"Oh," he says, frowning.

"I mean, I guess you can't really do that. It would take forever, and who knows what name she might have used," Maggie says.

"Susannah Myers…" I mumble.

"What?" Chase is totally out of his league with us.

"She likes the sound of my name—my maiden name, that is."

"Oh," he says and writes it down. It's hopeless. He'd never get anywhere with any of this nonsense. He knows it.

He looks at Maggie. "Do you have a sample of Casey's handwriting? I'd also like to see the note she wrote to you that you found this morning."

Maggie hesitates. "Oh. Of course. Let me go upstairs and get something she's written." She swallows hard and goes upstairs. *Chase isn't ruling out the possibility that Maggie has faked this note.* But why would she? She called in the missing persons report herself. He isn't skipping anything.

He glances at me as she walks around upstairs. "How's Myers?"

"He's fine."

"He come up with anything else?"

"No. I tried asking him again, but he seemed irritated that I was repeating your questions."

He nods. "Yeah." I watch as he looks over his notes.

"You think she's taken off, don't you?"

"It's looking that way. It's not unusual for kids to run away. Even though at age eighteen, we really wouldn't call it running away. Where do *you* think she would go?"

I shake my head. "I really have no idea. Maybe she went off with someone. If she really doesn't want to be found, she won't go anywhere we'd think to look."

"You're probably right," he says, shooting me one of those deep gazes. He shifts his eyes away, catching a glimpse of Maggie's computer screen and a smile begins.

"Is this you?"

"Oh! Yes. That's—what the red shoes were for. It's a book cover Maggie designed for one of her clients."

"Wow. That's impressive," he says, looking back at the screen as we hear her footsteps on the stairs.

Maggie is back with an old high school notebook and picks up the coffee filter off the dining room table. "Here's her AP English notebook, full of her handwriting. And this is the coffee filter."

Chase looks over the pages and compares the two samples, then glances at Maggie. "I'd like to take these back to the precinct. Our handwriting guy should take a look."

He's thorough if nothing else.

"Sure," says Maggie. "It's not looking like we're going to find her now, is it?"

"Well…Casey doesn't want to be found right now, it appears. But that's not to say she's run away forever. It seems from the tone of her note, and your previous good relationship with her, that she's planning on getting back in touch with you next week. Since she has college plans and a definite career path in front of her, I'd be really surprised if she'll stay out of touch for long."

Maggie takes a deep breath and sighs loudly. "I hope you're right."

"Still, I think you should keep tabs on her bank account, her Facebook page, and her phone records, and see if you can pick up a location. At least you might be able to pin down what city she's in. That could be a lead."

"So, you're saying you're off the case?"

"Not yet. Not today. I have a warrant to explore your phone records, so I've pulled up your cell phone records. On Casey's number there have been no calls made since Saturday. Several calls were made to her from you and Mr. French, but no calls out."

"I don't understand how she can communicate wherever she is without her cell phone."

Chase shrugs. "She could be using a burner phone so she can't be traced."

"That's pretty well thought out," I remark, making Maggie raise her eyebrows.

"I've also tapped into your Internet service, using that *88keys* password, but there has been no use of that by her since Saturday. Her browsing history hasn't turned up anything suspicious, other than some online shopping for shoes and music."

Maggie shrugs.

"She could also be going to the library and browsing to avoid leaving a trail," says Chase. "Or there's the simple possibility that there's no trail to be found."

"I hate to say this out loud," Maggie says, "but I never thought she was this clever."

"There's a lot out there to be learned from TV and movies and good detective novels. And our kids *are* the technology generation," Chase says.

"Which makes me wonder how she's doing this without her own convenient devices at hand."

"Like you said, she's smart. And she's apparently thought this through."

"I think she's with somebody and doesn't need to use any of it. What if somebody picked her up and took her off somewhere and she's just enjoying being detached from the world?" Maggie suggests.

"Can you blame her?" I say. "With all the pressure she's been under to get her life back on track, graduating, getting into college, and all these performances, maybe she just wanted to—stop the world for a while. *I would.*" Both of them nod at my comment.

"Maybe I should think of it as a vacation and hope she returns in time for school," says Maggie.

"And continue to be vigilant while she's gone. Don't forget, she said she'll call you next week, too," says Chase in a reassuring voice.

It dawns on me that this is the last we'll see of him, which is good in a way, but strangely, I don't want him to leave. His presence is reassuring in itself. I feel strangely off balance so I can only imagine how Maggie feels. When Casey gets in touch with Maggie, and it can't happen soon enough, I know everything will work out and things will get back to normal.

Normal. Whatever that is.

Chapter 10

THE LIST

Stan's arms are around me and he's whispering something in my ear. I laugh, but I don't really know what he said. When I open my eyes, I realize it's just a dream, and the arms wrapped around my middle are my own. There's nothing like reality to jolt you awake with a slap in the face. Irritably, I push my hands away from my body and stretch, now wide awake. I check the clock on the bedside table: 6:00 a.m. I haven't been for a run in several days due to the rain, and I've been exhausted with all the Casey drama going on. And now Stan is back? For once, I'm not happy to hear from him. It's been too long for my liking; he's hurt my feelings, like a boyfriend who didn't think enough of me to call. I definitely need to clear my head of this nonsense, I think, rubbing my eyes with the heels of my hands, and stretching. My empty-nester list needs some serious attention if I'm going to make it through my Stan withdrawal.

It's about time. What? Who is talking to me now? Huh, maybe it's just me.

I kick the covers aside and sit on the side of my bed to orient myself. Then I stand and stretch, gazing around my room to locate my running shorts and tank top, but they are nowhere in sight. Opening a drawer, I'm able to find what I need and dress slowly, allowing myself to wake up. Running shoes and socks in hand, I pad into the kitchen to start the coffee, put up my hair, and check the weather, seeing out the window that it's sunny and a hot day is in the making. It will be best to get on with my plans before it gets any hotter. I try to be at the office by 8:15 each morning so I'll have plenty of time to readjust my head for the day. As I watch the dark coffee swoosh and drip into the pot, I give Stan another chance to talk to me and then find myself rolling my eyes. He has left the building and it makes me angry. Was I truly deluding myself, trying to keep him around?

After a cup of coffee, a glass of water, slathering on my sunscreen, and doing some stretching on my front porch, I can hear my bird friends chirping to each other. Also, I can hear a distressed mewing sound and Mrs. Miller, my next-door neighbor, calling to Fang, her cat. He's on the roof again. Every so often Fang climbs the oak tree in her front yard, jumps across to the roof, and gets stranded, afraid to come back down. I smile to myself and watch as my elderly neighbor pats the tree and coaxes Fang to jump across and come down. It should be so simple; going down the same way he got up seems like a no-brainer. Why is it so hard for the poor little fellow?

Leaving my empty cup on the top step, I put on my weathered Carolina baseball cap and walk down the steps and go next door to see whether I can help. Mrs. Miller's white hair sticks out in odd whorls around the crown of her head, and her pink bathrobe is buttoned askew, as if she'd hurriedly dressed in her quest to rescue Fang.

"Good morning, Mrs. Miller," I say gently, hoping not to startle her.

"Oh! Hi, Dr. Brody! Fang's gotten himself stuck again."

"Aw! I thought so! Can I help you?"

"No…it'll just take him some time to get up his nerve and then he'll jump across and back himself on down. You'd think he'd be getting the hang of it by now. You going on a run?"

"Yeah. I haven't been in a while, and it's such a nice time of the morning."

"Mm-hmm, not so humid yet," she agrees and gestures to Fang to jump across to the tree. "Come on, little buddy! You can do it!"

"Meeaaooww!" cries Fang and sets himself to spring.

"Oh! Watch this!" she says with a little giggle. "Come on!" Fang jumps and lands, spread-eagle on the side of the tree, clinging for dear life with his claws, like a starfish on the sand.

"Yea!" we both shout and Mrs. Miller claps her hands, as if the cat is a baby who has just taken his first steps.

"Here he comes!" I say, watching the cat backing down the tree trunk, looking over his shoulder and yowling with each foot of progress he makes. His name hardly suits him since he appears to be such a wimp, and a cute, furry little one at that! In a few moments and with our cheer-leading, he is within reach so that Mrs. Miller can scoop him off the tree. He lands happily, purring in her arms.

"Wow! You don't see that every day." I reach up to stroke Fang's soft gray head.

"You should get a cat," she tells me. "They're wonderful company." I smile and shrug. Then, both of us turn, hearing the quick, pounding footsteps of a jogger on the sidewalk behind me, and we see Chase coming gradually to a halt in front of us. He slows his breathing and places his hands on his hips. There are already dark spots on his gray T-shirt around his chest and at his armpits. I try not to look at his legs, the way he did mine the other day.

"Morning! Fang get stuck again?"

"Yep. One of these days he'll learn to come down by himself, I hope," Mrs. Miller says and then turns to me. "Andrew was the one who helped me talk him down the first time. That was some fine police work, Detective," she laughs.

"Yeah, we thought we had a jumper on our hands, didn't we!" he says and they laugh.

Then he says to me suspiciously, "You're up and out early."

"Couldn't sleep. And I need to get myself in gear after all the—rain we've had." I was going to say *drama*, but I didn't want Mrs. Miller asking and then finding out that Casey was missing. Then again, she might know something. I hesitate, but I think better of it. *Casey is on vacation from life and will return when she's ready*, I tell myself. Chase doesn't say anything either, and it seems like he knows what I'm thinking. He winks at me, just slightly, and Mrs. Miller doesn't catch it.

"Well...have a good run. See you, Mrs. Miller!" he says, giving Fang's head a quick fondle and he's off again.

Mrs. Miller is looking at me with her eyebrows on alert, which means the same as, *You should get yourself a detective. They're wonderful company*, so I take that as my cue to skedaddle. I can feel my own eyebrows ratcheting up a notch in response to her look.

"Okay, I'm off too. Have a good day, Mrs. Miller. I'm glad Fang made it back to earth safely!"

"Bye-bye!" she sings out, waving Fang's paw at me.

I hit the sidewalk at a brisk pace, heading the opposite direction from Chase. We may intersect again at some point, but my short run will be over before his, no doubt. I breathe deeply, inhaling the fragrance of freshly mown grass. Like the breathing of a warm summer morning, the crickets begin a chorus that rises and falls, and I am comforted at last. Why did I put this off for so many days? Routine is often the soul's savior, something I've known for three years. Loosening up, I swing my arms back and forth in front of me as I run. The rhythm of my feet begins a cadence in my head, making me wish I'd remembered my headphones and music, but I am soon happy to listen to the birds and insects as I cruise by the park.

Thirty minutes later and no sign of Chase, I am back at my front porch. I climb the steps and retrieve my glass of water. As soon as I walk inside, I am aware that Myers is up and moving about in the kitchen. I find him, standing at the island, drinking iced tea and spreading peanut butter on a bagel, his hair wet and combed, fresh from a shower. I refill my glass from the tap and drink eagerly.

"Hey! You're up early. What's up?"

"Mrs. Sullivan called. She wants me to watch Danny and Hayden this morning. She's got an early tennis match and then she's planning on having lunch with her buds afterward."

"Oh, okay. What are you going to do with the boys?" Myers makes good money babysitting many of the boys in Magnolia. Responsible boy babysitters are hard to come by.

He chews a moment, pointing to his violin case on the table. "They wanted a violin lesson, but that will be after swim team practice."

"Good for you! Your bank account must be growing steadily."

"Yup!" he grins.

"How was open mike last night?"

"Great! I met another person interested in having me play at a wedding. It's in August right before I head off to school."

"Excellent!" I say, glancing at the growing stack of mail. Maybe I'll go through it…tonight.

"Did Maggie hear anything about Casey?"

"Oh, yeah. I guess I haven't told you all the details. Maggie found a note Casey'd left. It was written on a coffee filter and it said she's okay but not to look for her. She'll call next week."

He squints. "A coffee filter? That's random."

"I guess Casey knew she'd go in that cupboard the next day. Maybe she did it to buy herself some time. What do you think?"

"I think it's weird. Is that detective still looking for her, then?"

"I don't think so. He had warrants to investigate further, but now it seems apparent that she's taking a little break and will come back when she's ready."

"That's probably right. Well, I'm gonna go on over to the Sullivans' house. I'll see you tonight."

"Okay. I'm going to Pilates class after work, so we'll have lasagna when I get back, okay? I have some in the freezer, so we can eat late."

"Awesome!" he grins. Lasagna is his favorite. I want to keep feeding him as long as he's around, but I could pass on the calories, myself. The things we do for love. I guess I will sacrifice myself! "Guess you're back to the bucket list?"

"Yeah. It feels good, too." I think about signing up for the sailing class in the fall. *Wonder who you could meet?* says a voice in my head. Wow. Where did that come from? I must be talking to myself now. It's definitely not Stan.

"What's wrong?" Myers asks, picking up his violin off the counter.

"Nothing, why?"

"You just had a funny look on your face."

"So do you half the time."

He cocks his head and crosses his eyes, sticking out his tongue sideways for effect. His cell phone rings from his pocket. It's back to the old ring I remember.

I laugh, "Go on! Laura Sullivan is probably wondering where you are."

"Okay. See you later," he says, retrieving the phone to answer the call.

"Have a good day!"

He nods to me as he answers his phone on his way out the back door.

I check the time and dash through my bedroom to the shower. I'm going to be late.

Maggie is late to class, but I am actually surprised she is here at all, with so much on her mind. She takes a spot next to me and I watch her during our warm-up stretches. She looks exhausted. Dark rings under her eyes are always a giveaway that she's worried. I will have to wait until after class to see what's on her mind.

"Any news?" I ask, wiping sweat off my face when class is over.

She looks pensive. "No, but I was looking back through Casey's Facebook messages from friends whose names I didn't know."

"What'd you find out?"

"There are so many people she knows from all her camps and music intensives she's attended. There must be fifty different kids who live in other places that have told her, 'Let's stay in touch' or 'Come and see me.' I'll never get through the list."

"Never say 'never.' Any cute guys on the list?"

"Yeah, there were a couple. One was *really* good-looking and just her type. They've communicated quite a bit. He's going to college in the fall too, but it's not South Carolina. I stalked a profile or two and then I left to come here. That's why I was late."

"Want to come over for dinner? Myers and I are having lasagna," I say, trying to tempt her.

"Oh, thanks, but Ed is back home and we're meeting some friends for dinner at the Raw Bar."

"He's back?"

"Yes, for the Fourth."

"Oh, right!" I'd forgotten that tomorrow is the Fourth of July. Who in her right mind forgets a holiday? Maybe I'm more preoccupied than I thought. "Do you and Ed have plans?"

"Yes, our friends Joanne and Bob have invited us to Lake Norman for the day. They always spend the night on their sailboat, so we're going to join them and watch the fireworks. I think Ed's trying to keep me busy; you know, to take my mind off Casey. And you know Ed—he never misses a party."

"That sounds like fun." I miss couples' events like that since I seldom get invited anymore. I'm not a couple.

"What are you and Myers doing?"

"I don't know. Usually we picnic with Mom and Dad and watch the neighborhood parade and the fireworks. He and I haven't even talked about it, and with Mom and Dad being so sick, I'm not sure they'll be up for it."

"What's wrong?"

"They were sick when they came back from China."

"Oh, no! Is it serious?"

"Well, they've picked up respiratory infections, but they went to their doctor and got medicated, so hopefully they'll be better soon. At their age, they don't take any chances, and they've been smart, staying home, resting, and eating their chicken soup."

"Good for them. I hope they feel better."

We are standing in front of our cars in the parking lot. "Well, call me if you hear anything."

"You know I will," she says, giving me a sweaty hug, but I don't care because I'm sweatier than she is.

Myers is home when I arrive. I expect to hear him playing his violin like he does most evenings, but I find him out in the garage, rummaging around in one of the storage bins. On the floor are his sleeping bag and two-man tent. The backpack comes out next, which he sets carefully on the floor.

"Hey! What's going on?" He doesn't even look up.

"I'm getting out my camping equipment. Tim and I are thinking about going camping for a few days up in the Smokies. Would you be okay with that?"

My Eagle Scout can disappear for days in the mountains, but even though I know he is fully capable of taking care of himself, I still worry when he's gone.

"When are you planning to go?"

This time he looks up and wipes his nose on the back of his hand from the dust in the garage. "Tomorrow."

"But…tomorrow's the Fourth."

"I know. That's why Tim can get away. The bank will be closed, and he's asked for Friday off, so that gives him Saturday and Sunday off too." Tim had the good fortune to land a bank teller's job in the village after graduation.

"Well…"

"Do you mind?"

"I guess not," I say, shrugging, trying not to show that my feelings are hurt. I might well be spending the day alone, so maybe I should just start sucking it up and get used to it. Myers looks guilty.

"Aren't you going to spend the day with Dandy and Mima anyway?"

"Yeah, probably, if they're feeling up to it. I need to call them…."

He doesn't try to back out, and I don't want him to.

"I just figure...you know, that Tim and I won't have many more chances to go before school starts. And the weather looks good, so..." he says with a shrug of his own.

"No, it's fine. You should go," I say, dismissing his reservations. I doubt he really cares to hang around for fireworks. I remember losing touch with my friends too, once I left for college. He resumes packing his car, so I go back inside and retrieve the lasagna from the freezer and preheat the oven. The door is still open to the garage so I call out to him, "Hey, will you put this in the oven when it beeps?"

"Sure," he calls back.

"Thanks! I'm going to hop in the shower real quick, okay? Then I'll make us a salad." Asking him to set the timer would be too much to ask, so I'll have to keep track of the time. He's on his phone again anyway, so I go back to my bedroom to shower and change.

I call to check on Mom and Dad before we sit down to dinner. They still haven't recovered from their illnesses so I will be on my own for the holiday. They don't even need dinner. Their church friends have been bringing over food. I am of no use to anyone, it seems. Myers disappears to his bedroom after dinner and is strangely silent. No violin concert for me tonight. He is probably watching movies on his computer. I force myself to go through the mail and spend an hour playing the piano—Vivaldi, in hopes that the energetic melodies will cheer me up. Finally, I give up and go back to my bedroom, put on my pajamas, and climb in bed. Maybe I'll read, I think, looking over the selections stacked on my bedside table. I pick up the book on top.

Stan the Man.

Chapter 11

ON HOLIDAY

I hear Myers up before six o'clock. That hour is highly irregular for my teenage son, even for beginning a camping trip. He must be putting his food together, I think, as I emerge slowly from my bedroom wrapped in my own bathrobe, trying to focus my eyes. This is supposed to be my holiday, and I was hoping to sleep in since I didn't fall asleep until the wee hours of this morning. Crossly, I watch Myers spreading peanut butter and jelly on oatmeal bread in the kitchen.

"That's all you're taking?" I ask, noticing there is no other food around.

He looks up at me, as if I have caught him red-handed.

"Oh, hey. I didn't hear you come in."

I go immediately to the coffeepot and take a filter out of my cabinet, finding myself checking it for any notes from my son! As I scoop coffee into the basket, I try to make Myers talk to me. Although he is up early today, he is not a morning person.

"You're leaving awfully early. Will Tim be up?"

"That was the plan," he says in his soft half-voice. He isn't quite awake yet either.

The coffee begins to drip as I lean against the counter to look at him.

"So where exactly are you going?" I ask, rubbing my eyes.

"We're going up on the Appalachian Trail, near Roan Mountain," he says, packing another sandwich into a plastic bag. He fills his water bottle from the water dispenser on the refrigerator.

"Will you call me when you get up there, so I'll know where you are?"

"Sure. I might not always have good phone reception up there, so you might not be able to reach me, but I'll keep in touch."

"Is this all the food you're taking?" I ask, pouring coffee into my favorite mug and stirring in sugar and creamer.

"That's Tim's department since I'm driving."

"Oh. Just the two of you going?"

"Yeah."

As I sip my coffee, I watch him collecting his few items and reaching for his keys.

"Are you all packed up, then?"

"Yep. I should be back Sunday, if not before then."

"Okay," I say, watching him turn toward the door.

"Hey, where's my hug?"

"Oh, sorry, Mom," he says, coming to embrace me. "Bye, Mom."

"Bye, kiddo. Have fun. Be careful. And don't forget to call me. I know a detective, you know," I laugh, poking my finger in his chest.

He snorts, giving me a look. He is out the door when I notice his blue windbreaker hanging on the hook in the laundry room. "Hey, Myers? Aren't you going to need your jacket? It gets cold up there even in the summer, right?"

He looks surprised. "Oh. Yeah. Thanks. I thought I'd put it in the car already. I have other stuff packed." He walks back to get his jacket and is out the door with another "Bye, Mom" and is in his car as I wave. I watch him back out of the garage, nosing his SUV down the street; then I turn back inside. I hate that he's developed the habit of not looking back when he goes away. My baby is all grown up.

I finish my coffee at the sink and decide, since I am up, that I might as well get my morning run out of the way. If I can stay awake until the fireworks are over, I can go to bed early. People will sit out in the park to watch. I can watch the parade and see the show from my porch, so I don't even have to leave the house. What an old fuddy-duddy I'm becoming!

Sighing, I go to my room to dress for my run. After pulling a bright pink tank top over my head and putting my black shorts on, I make it to the front porch steps to sit down and put on my socks and shoes and apply my sunscreen. It's another beautiful morning, so I need to stop feeling sorry for myself and let Mother Nature take me under her nurturing wing. Breathing deeply while I stretch my calves, I can smell Mrs. Miller's gardenias as the morning mist begins to lift. They are heaven! I close my eyes and breathe again and jump as I feel something soft brush my leg. My eyes fly open and there is Fang, his lithe gray body sliding past my thigh as he begins to purr loudly. I had no idea cats could make so much noise.

"Good morning!" I greet him, stroking his sweet head; he pushes it toward my hand, making me laugh. I wonder whether Mrs. Miller would let me rent him. He *would* make good company when Myers leaves. "What are you doing here? Where's your mother?" I'm talking to a cat. I don't know what to do with him actually, and I wonder whether I should take him back over to my neighbor's house before he ventures over to her roof again. That would be the responsible thing to do, rather than running off into the morning and having him on the loose. Come to think of it, Fang has never wandered onto my porch in all the time I've lived here.

He lets me lift him into my arms and meows at me, pushing his nose into my chin, his whiskers tickling my neck. "Okay, home you go, friend." As I carry Fang down my steps and turn the corner toward Mrs.

Miller's house, I can see through her storm door that her front door is open. It usually stays open when she lets Fang out during the day, while she keeps the storm door shut to keep in the cool air. Her newspaper is still on the sidewalk, so I stoop to pick it up and settle it in my arms with Fang. We go up her walkway and up the front porch steps. He is much heavier than I'd thought. I knock on the door and wait, but there is no answer. I ring the bell, but Mrs. Miller doesn't come to the door. Maybe she is out in the backyard, tending her flowers. Her dahlias are just beginning to bloom and she is quite proud of them. Fang squirms in my arms and jumps down, slipping deftly through the cat door.

"Fine," I mutter, brushing hair off my arms as he struts off. Cats are so fickle. Then I have a discomforting thought. *Something isn't right.* Forgetting about the backyard, I step back to the door where I can peer inside. Seeing no movement, I test the door to see whether it's locked. It gives when I push down the latch and I am able to step inside.

"Mrs. Miller?" I call, but there is no answer. I step inside and walk slowly through the foyer to the kitchen where I can hear labored breathing. Hurrying around the counter, I first see the embroidered toe of a blue bedroom slipper and then Mrs. Miller's figure crumpled on the floor. "Oh! Mrs. Miller, can you hear me?" I cry out, looking for a telephone. I grab it from its cradle on the counter before sinking next to her on the floor. She is barely conscious, but she tries to speak. Already I can tell that one side of her face is not working, and she is pale and unable to move her limbs. Her eyes dart about fearfully. Immediately, I call 911. "It's all right, Mrs. Miller. I'm going to get some help. Can you talk?"

She murmurs incoherently, her lips trying to form words and sounds to no avail. As I wait for the dispatcher to answer the phone, that eerie softness floats past my leg again and I realize Fang's presence. "Thanks, buddy. Mrs. Miller, I think Fang came to get me," I laugh, trying to calm her while we wait. Finally, the dispatcher answers and asks about my emergency.

I tell her I think Mrs. Miller has suffered a stroke. I give what I think is her age and general medical condition, but without any knowledge of her personally, I can't give the dispatcher much more than the address and that my neighbor is conscious, unable to speak or move, and I promise that I haven't and will not attempt to move her. I stay on the line for what seems like an hour before I can make out sirens. Watching her constantly, I make a quick detour into her living room, find a chenille throw to put over her to keep her warm and hold her hand until the EMTs are shortly at my side, beginning their assessment and triage. I step away as one of them asks me more questions I can't answer. The other man talks gently to Mrs. Miller, but loud enough in case she is hard of hearing. I reassure them that she has very good hearing. I scan the kitchen and find a red address book and a cell phone, scrolling through her contacts, looking for emergency numbers. Another glance around her kitchen rewards me with more of Mrs. Miller's good planning. She has left a note listing her current medications on her refrigerator under a magnet! I remove it and hand it to one of the men in charge. In a short time, the paramedics have settled Mrs. Miller onto a gurney and are preparing to load her into the ambulance. I have found a phone number for her son, whom I've only met once and seen a time or two. He lives in Columbia, an hour and a half away, but I place a call and he answers on the second ring. I explain who I am and what is happening with his mother. He is concerned and grateful for the call. I ask one of the paramedics which hospital they will be taking her to and he tells me Presbyterian in Charlotte, so I relay the information to Mark Miller and tell him I will follow them there, giving him my cell phone number in case he needs a contact.

"Mrs. Miller, I just talked to Mark," I say, looking at her for signs of comprehension, and thankfully, she nods and closes her eyes. "He's on his way and will meet you at the hospital. I'm going to meet you there too, okay?" I pat her arm as she is being loaded into the back of the truck and the doors close. I run back into the house and find her keys on a hook near the back door. I lock the front door of her house as the ambulance lights begin to spin.

I dash back to my house and grab my own keys and my purse. Carefully, I back my car out of the garage, and in my hurry, almost run over a figure crossing the sidewalk. *"Shit!"* I cry out, slamming on the brakes.

It's Chase, on his morning run. My window buzzes down and I call out my apologies.

"What happened? I heard the ambulance," he says, looking worried and out of breath, as if he's kicked it into high gear to get here. He bends at the waist, resting his hands on his knees so he can hear me—and catch his breath.

"It's Genevieve Miller. It looks like she's had a stroke. Her cat came and got me, and I went over there and found her lying on the floor...."

His anxious face softens, imagining Fang coming to the rescue, or maybe because I've stated it like that. "Way to go, Fang!" he says breathlessly.

I gesture quickly with my hand, trying to illustrate there is no time to waste chit-chatting on the sidewalk. "I'm going. Presbyterian," I say and peel out of my driveway in my Prius, gunning it around the corner, looking for the ambulance, which is barely visible on the road ahead.

"Wait!" I hear Chase yell, and I hit the brakes, realizing he is hauling ass behind my car! How bizarre! "Let me go with you!" he says, jerking open the door and jumping into the passenger seat.

Tires squeal as I try to catch up with the ambulance.

He laughs. "Okay, Danica! Didn't you say they were going to Presbyterian?"

"Yeah, but they could get diverted and go somewhere else and then we'd be sitting there in the wrong hospital like fools and her son will think I'm a total idiot."

"Huh. Yeah, you're right. They went that-a-way," he says in his charming drawl, throwing a thumb to the left. There is only one way out of the village and out onto the highway toward Charlotte, so it's doubtful I could really lose the ambulance or the bright red fire truck that is following it back out onto the main street.

I blush in spite of the effort not to, and I can feel Chase laughing silently beside me. "I guess this is more your thing."

"Chasing ambulances? Nah, not really. I leave that to the two-bit lawyers most of the time," he says, rubbing a hand down his forearm, wiping off sweat from his run. *Two-bit lawyers like my ex-husband,* looking for desperate DUI offenders to represent. There won't be a thing Kent can do for them, except to describe in the most graphic detail what will most likely happen to them, giving them the best and worst case scenarios, while charging them at least a thousand bucks. Not a bad gig for a couple of hours' time and pushing around some paperwork. And he hires a paralegal to push the paperwork around. In a city the size of Charlotte, five poor chumps like that a day and one can make a pretty decent living. Conscience optional.

"Are you working today?" I ask, thinking Chase really doesn't have time for this.

"Actually, I am, but since it's a holiday—for most people, at least—I can be late and it's no big deal. On the Fourth of July, most people save their bad behavior for later on in the evening." He turns to me and I can smell his sunscreen, as I am trained to do. Sweat has darkened the hair around his temples. "I usually put in overtime anyway."

I know this also. "Well, Mrs. Miller will be overwhelmed with her neighbors' attentions."

"How was she when you saw her?"

"Trying to talk a little, but her speech was incomprehensible, although she seemed to understand what was going on. She wasn't moving, but then I made her lie still until the EMTs arrived."

"Good thing you're a doctor and handled it so well."

"How could you possibly tell that?"

"You're cool and collected. Not many people would be so calm under pressure."

"Thank you." *I almost ran over you!* Really cool.

"Were you able to contact her family?"

"Yes. I found an emergency number for her son in her phone, and I verified it in her address book on the kitchen counter. And I found a list of her meds stuck to her fridge."

"Ah…good detective work."

"It must be rubbing off on me."

"So the son is…?"

"He's coming. He was getting ready to jump in the car and drive up here from Columbia."

"That's good. Good work. It's nice of you to go to the hospital with her."

"Like you are, too."

"Well…I figure if it were my mama, I'd want somebody taking charge," he says, glancing at me from the corner of his eye.

"You're going to be really late for work. I won't leave her until Mark gets to the hospital. That's two hours max."

"It's okay. The department's getting me on a holiday. I can call my own shots."

By this time, we are on the interstate and I am almost at the exit. Fortunately, there is none of the usual morning traffic due to the hour and the holiday. My satellite radio is playing a country song that Chase taps his thumb to on the side of his naked leg. I haven't sat in a car next to a man near my age whose leg I've seen uncovered in quite some time. It's oddly familiar—so oddly familiar and distracting that I almost miss my exit.

"I never have a smooth ride into the city like this," he says, turning the air conditioning down in my car, like he belongs here, as I'm power-sliding into the exit lane, but he doesn't react negatively. "Except early on Saturday mornings. Patti and I used to get up early sometimes on Saturdays and come in to the farmers market."

"Really?" *Stan and I used to do the same thing during the summers.* "We used to do that too. For the tomatoes."

"Yeah, the tomatoes and cantaloupes. Patti loved cantaloupe. *Ambrosia*," he murmurs, as if I am not in the car. But I know the variety of cantaloupe he means. I like that one, too. It's the sweetest.

"You don't garden?" I ask, feeling as though I want him in the present.

"No. No time. You?"

"No. And I love going to the farmers market. It's a lot cheaper and faster than growing your own." *Stan used to buy me flowers at the farmers market.* Now who's not present? I'm drifting…we're walking hand-in-hand through the market, sipping coffee….

I've caught every green light and find that we are approaching the hospital before I know it. Chase shows me which entrance to take, and of course, I remember. "This is where I brought Myers when he got kicked in the throat during a soccer game ten years ago," I murmur, as if to myself, but I want him to know. *And where I met the love of my life.*

"Is that why his voice always sounds a little hoarse?"

I nod. I feel the need to share with him, after he's said Patti liked cantaloupes. He probably thinks about her all the time, the same way I think about Stan. All the time.

"I met my husband here that day."

"He was a doctor, wasn't he?"

"Yes. He worked in the emergency department. It was a slow day and he treated Myers. Normally, Stan would have been treating the trauma cases, but it was ten in the morning, so he was free," I explain, pulling into a parking place and turning off the engine. Chase seems to be listening intently, but then, that's what he does best.

The conversation is over as we enter through the Emergency Room doors and request the whereabouts of Genevieve Miller. She has arrived and has been admitted to the triage area, where the staff is treating her. Even though we are not family, the charge nurse allows us back to be with Mrs. Miller. Both of us touch her hands as we greet her to reassure her that she's not alone. I explain to the doctor in charge that we are neighbors and that Mark, her son, is on the way from Columbia. At the doctor's request, I explain what happened and how I found her when I saw her on her kitchen floor. After reviewing her vital signs and her meds with the EMTs, the doctor orders a CAT scan, so I give Mrs. Miller's hand a squeeze. Since this is the first time Chase has seen Mrs. Miller after her stroke, I watch a worried look cross his face, an unusual show of emotion for him, touching me surprisingly.

"We're right outside, okay? Mark is on his way and we'll stay until he gets here."

Mrs. Miller nods and closes her eyes. The ER techs take over her gurney and they disappear through swinging double doors on the way to the CAT lab. The nurse directs us to have a seat in the waiting room.

Already, several people are waiting in the large, fluorescently lit room. An older man sits under the TV, texting, oblivious to us, and a young couple watches us come in. Another man curses into his cell phone about how the ER patient he is with is inconveniencing him as he paces near the TV. We sit in the cleanest chairs we can find. Under the stare of the couple who continues to watch us, I am acutely aware that I am under-dressed for the occasion in my running clothes. Chase looks unaffected by his own appearance, so I try to stop worrying about mine and turn my attention to calling Mrs. Miller's son on his cell phone. We chat for a moment and he tells me he is only forty minutes away.

"He must be flying," Chase says when I report this.

"Well, it's his mama, like you said."

We sit in silence for a moment. Chase sits forward and rests his elbows on his knees, then turns to me. "So, do you know Mrs. Miller very well?"

"Somewhat. She…was so kind to Myers and me when Stan died. And even before that, when Myers would walk home from elementary school when he was old enough to be a latchkey kid, she'd watch out for him until I got home. He'd feed her cat when she went out of town, which has been less and less lately. How about you? She must mean something to you too, seeing as how you were trying to run and leap into my car like Superman!"

He chuckles, rubbing the palms of his hands together. "Mrs. Miller was my casserole queen when Patti died."

The familiar thought makes me smile, and we say in unison, "Chicken tetrazzini!"

"I used to toss her newspaper up to her front porch on my morning runs, and one day she caught me doing it. She asked me if I was her personal paperboy!"

"She's a funny lady." I giggle at the image, thinking about how at her advanced age, Mrs. Miller still likes to flirt.

"Everybody needs a little humor," he says, sitting back in the chair.

"Yes…I think Maggie French could use a little humor about now."

"Absolutely. Have you talked to her?"

"Not since last night. She's still overwhelmed with how many people Casey seems to know."

"So, what's Casey really like?" he asks, folding his hands across his stomach.

I laugh. "Do you remember the first time you ever poured a diet soda into a glass too fast and the fizz shot up out of the glass?" He nods. "That's Casey. Overly effervescent and a total surprise."

"Why is she a surprise?" he cocks his head.

"She just seems so…*ordinary* on first glance, but she's anything but ordinary."

"But she and Maggie get along well?"

"Yeah. But living with Casey is like trying to catch the wind. It's more her dad who likes to butt heads with her. Not in a bad way. They just see things differently. But he's mentored her all her life. He was a concert pianist and now teaches. He wants her to follow in his footsteps. Anyway, Maggie's sick about her disappearance. I think even though she doesn't say it, she's beating herself up over whatever it was that made Casey leave."

"I think she probably just wanted to break out of Magnolia."

I nod. "I'm sure Myers feels the same way, but he's getting his chance in August. And so would Casey, but for her now, it's not the same thing."

"Yeah, I imagine going to school in Nashville will be like stepping into heaven for him. He must be really talented."

"He is. I realize it more and more every time I see him perform. His talent grows exponentially."

"Must be nice, knowing what you're born to do at such an early age."

There is a comfortable silence as we observe the cursing man being called back to the ER to visit his not-so-loved one.

"What do you think Myers knows?"

"What do you mean?"

"I don't think he was telling me everything when we talked. You know him best. What's he holding back?"

"You think he's lying." It's not a question, and strangely, I'm not upset about his suspicions.

"If he's lying, he's doing it to protect Casey. I think he knows where she is. I don't think she's in any danger, either, or he'd definitely tell you." His green eyes turn to me, making me feel that annoying frisson of vulnerability when someone slips inside your soul, uninvited. Then it occurs to me that Chase has hitched a ride to pump me for information about my son. Maybe he's not late for work at all. Maybe he's working me right now. He's still looking at me with that earnest expression. He has mastered his craft brilliantly. I will not be swayed by his apparent charms.

I can feel my eyes narrowing at him. "Are you still on the case?"

"I shouldn't be. I should turn in the warrants and spend my time on my other cases. But I'm a dad, too, and if Olivia was MIA, I'd want somebody to help me find her."

So I overreacted maybe. He continues.

"Look, it's natural to be defensive when someone accuses your son of lying. I just think Casey is okay, but still—it's nerve-wracking playing the waiting game." Okay, so I've misjudged him completely. Maybe. He's a detective so his motivations are hard to discern. My gut feeling is that Chase is just a nice guy with no agenda.

Maybe.

"I know. I didn't mean to sound ungrateful. Maggie appreciates your help. We all do. I'm not naïve enough to think Myers has never lied to me. I lied all the time when I was his age, so my parents wouldn't be disappointed in the dumb things I was doing. And I have to admit, Myers can stonewall you at times."

"He's definitely got his guard up.... You and Maggie seem really close."

"She's my best friend." *The sister I should have had.* "She and I have known each other since our kids were eight years old. When Myers started taking violin lessons, I couldn't get him to his classes since I was working, so Maggie would pick him up after school, bring him a snack, and take him to his lessons. Myers would never be where he is without her." I'm about to mention how Maggie helped me through Stan's death when the charge nurse pages me.

"Mrs. Brody?" she asks and gestures to a short, stout, harried man about my age, standing at the desk, slipping his driver's license back into his wallet. He looks vaguely familiar.

"Oh, you must be Mark Miller. I'm Susannah Brody, your mom's next door neighbor," I say, extending my hand in greeting. "Hi."

"Hi! Yes, I'm Mark. I've seen you before. My wife Brenda is parking our car. I can't thank you enough for taking care of Mom and contacting me. How in the world did you discover her?"

As I tell the story about Fang appearing mysteriously on my porch, a short, stout, blond-haired woman in a red, white, and blue shirt with white crop pants, red sandals and matching fingernails comes flying through the ER doors, and Mark introduces me to Brenda. She was ready for the holiday picnic apparently, and she gazes distractedly at my running clothes, making me wish I'd grabbed a jacket. *It's freezing in here!* I stand close by, rubbing my arms and listening to the updates on where Mrs. Miller is in the hospital. She is back from her CAT scan and resting in the ER, so the charge nurse invites Mark and Brenda to go back where they can be with her. They turn to say goodbye to me and Chase, who has now joined the group and introduced himself. After shaking hands all around, they promise they'll keep us updated, wrongly assuming we are a couple, judging from our attire and possibly our wedding bands. Neither of us bothers to explain, and as I hand over Mrs. Miller's keys, we leave them at the door where the no-nonsense nurse takes over.

Back in the car, we begin to relax, and Chase cranks up the air as I back out of the parking place. On with the day. On with the Fourth of July, and on with the heat. I'm hot now. My quest for exercise can wait until tomorrow, or later this evening, after the sun goes down. I have never been on a run under the accompaniment of fireworks. I'll have to add that to my bucket list. It may become a tradition. Chase must be thinking ahead as well.

"So, what are you doing for the holiday?"

"Uh, cleaning my house and…I don't know. Not much," I reply, suddenly embarrassed to admit I have nothing to do.

"Not doing anything with Myers?"

"No. He's gone camping with a friend. How about you? You're working. Aren't your kids home for the summer?"

"No. Ryan's working a summer internship in Charleston and Olivia's at my sister's house out in California." He has been alone longer than I have. Maybe I can pick up some tips on how he manages.

"Oh, really? How is Olivia?"

"She's great. She's working in my sister's bakery. Did it last summer, too. Karen, my sister, and her husband Doug, live in a little town on the coast called Pacific Grove. Karen wants me to move out there," he says, scraping the side of one thumb with the other absently.

"Would you move, all that way?"

"Eh…it's a small town, but a beautiful place. There's not much action as far as the police force is concerned. But maybe whenever there's an opening, it could work. But then my kids would lose their in-state tuition at Carolina. I might consider it when they're both out of college and settled."

"Do you miss them?"

"Yeah. It's insanely quiet around my house."

"Mine, too, and getting quieter all the time."

"Yeah, it'll be real quiet when Myers leaves. He's your only child?"

"Yes."

"Well, I can imagine your practice keeps you pretty busy."

"It's gotten that way. When I started in the village, I wasn't sure I was going to make it, but then, it's like the whole thing just exploded. Now, it's gotten so that people don't understand why they have to wait a week or more to book an appointment."

"It's nice to be in demand," he says, giving me an encouraging look. He's quiet a moment, and I can sense a new tension in the air. "So, if you're not doing anything, I'm icing down a watermelon at the house. Would you like to share it with me later and watch some fireworks?"

His invitation catches me off-guard. My shocked face and obvious hesitation deflate his momentum, so he back-pedals immediately.

"Well, I mean, I don't know what time I'll get through at the precinct, but hopefully, it will be before anything explodes in the sky."

I laugh. "It's just that…I thought I might need to check in on my parents." *God, that sounds so lame!* "They've been sick, and I just want to make sure they're okay."

"Absolutely. No problem," he says, letting me completely off the hook. Damn! And I have to drive him all the way back home. I should have pretended not to hear him when he yelled for me as I peeled around the corner. *What am I, thirteen?* We are both staring at our own wedding rings. Aren't we a pair? *Sure, and I'll bring the fried chicken and some potato salad,* is what I should be saying. Chase is a nice guy, a really decent guy, and Genevieve Miller has all but thrown us together. Suddenly, the thought of her faking her apparent stroke in the guise of matchmaking for us sends me into a little spill of laughter.

"What is it?" he says.

"I don't know. I just thought of something silly. It's nothing," I say, but I think I've really wounded him; not that he appears to be sulking, but I can tell. Is it too late to take him up on his invitation? And then I get an image of Chase and Patti, strolling hand-in-hand through the farmers market, stopping to thump watermelons, checking them for ripeness…. *Oh, God! What am I even thinking?* At that moment, the driver in the truck in front of me slams on his brakes, making me do the same, jolting us out of our topic. The twisted black remains of a tire, like an anaconda stretched across the road, appears to be the cause of the almost-accident, making me swallow and try to focus on getting us home in one piece.

"Sorry," I say, followed by a long exhale.

"The heat must have caused someone's tire to disintegrate," he says, glad to have the topic steered away from the dating disaster we were headed for. We spend the rest of the drive in silence until we head down the main street of Magnolia Village.

"Where do you live?" I ask, as it dawns on me that I have no idea. Patti and I never visited each other. Being the busy mothers we were, we only saw each other at Pilates class.

"I'm on the other side of the park from you, on Summer Walk."

In a moment, we are at his street, and he directs me to turn left, away from the park. I could throw a rock to his house from mine. His place is neat, although the front porch could use flowerpots, maybe some ferns hanging from the rafters, and maybe a wreath—all women's touches.

He places a hand on the door handle as I pull up in front of his house. He turns to me and I squeeze my eyes shut for an instant, thinking he's going to pursue the date thing again. But he surprises me.

"What about Fang? He'll need to be fed and taken care of."

"Yes. Yes, he will. And kept off the roof," I laugh, relieved that's all that's on his mind. "I'll call Mark and ask him what their plans are. I have Mrs. Miller's spare key, so I can take care of him, until she comes back…" I say, and both of us are wondering whether she will, or how long it might be.

"Okay. Thanks for letting me *ride along*," Chase says, and I think he's just winked at me.

"Sure. Bye," I say, as he hoists himself out of my car and holds the door for a moment.

"Take care, Susannah," he says.

I watch him bound up the steps to his porch.

Damn!

Chapter 12

A DATE-NOT

It's been a good day at the office. My skyrocket run in the dark last night was quite a liberating and joyful experience, and I thought it was rather apropos, pursuing life, liberty, and happiness all by myself on our nation's birthday. Maybe it was just the all around good night's sleep I had, but I feel rejuvenated today; that, and the fact that my patients are so sweet. Mr. Quinlan brought me a big hunk of his wife's lemon pound cake, left over from their neighborhood picnic, and the first tomatoes from his garden. He certainly knows how to woo his doctor! Mrs. Sanford brought me a bottle of moisturizer with sunscreen, my favorite kind of product. It's a new one she's selling for a company she represents, and she wants my evaluation of it so she can recommend it to her clients. Mr. Rosen stayed past his appointed time, telling us all his new jokes, and had Rosetta, my nurse, and me in stitches. *"Which color thread would you like for me to sew you up with?" asked the dermatologist. "Suture self,"* *replied the patient!* And then he asks if it's normal to sweat as much as he does. *I'm a big sweater. I come from a long line of sweaters. My father was a turtleneck!* We're still laughing as we finish up our patient notes on our computer tablets. I'm hanging up my lab coat on the back of my office door when my cell phone rings. It's Chase. I freeze for a second. Then I relax. Maybe he has more information about Casey.

"Hello?"

"Susannah, it's Chase. Hey, are you still at work?"

"Yes. I was just about to leave, actually. Do you have any news about Casey?"

"Nothing I can report, and neither does Maggie. I've checked in with her already. Listen—I—I'm sorry if I came out of the blue at you yesterday, asking you over for watermelon." I feel terrible at the way it sounds.

"Oh. No, it's fine. I'm the one who should be sorry. I should have offered to bring the fried chicken. I was…just tired, I think. I haven't been sleeping very well lately."

"I'm sorry. And I know the feeling. If I don't run every day, I'm up all night."

"And no caffeine for me after 10:00 a.m."

"Right," he says. I didn't expect him to agree with me. It's hard for me to imagine a cop not drinking coffee all day, but I'm sure Chase has his reasons. And they probably have to do with Patti. My pause allows him to go on.

"So, is there any possibility of getting a rain-check?"

A rain-check? Is he really asking me out? If I even dared to dream I'd be getting a second chance, he has blown me out of the water. *What is there to think about?* I inhale as inaudibly as I can and decide to be brave. "I think it's a possibility."

"Then, how about a neutral location, in case you need to bolt?"

"Oh, was I that bad?"

"Look, I can totally understand where you're coming from. And we don't have to call it a…date, or whatever. I haven't been out with someone in over two years. And I haven't had a first date since 1988, so…."

154

A date. I chuckle, unable to think of what to say.

"Jeez…how'm I doin'?" I can imagine him running a nervous hand over his hair.

"You're doing fine." His insecurity is somehow reassuring. Both of us are bad at this. "So when do you want to have this *date-not?*"

"Well, I'm in Charlotte, following up on some leads for a case I'm on. Are you at all free? I know it's really short notice, but would you care to meet me over here for a drink? Or I could just meet you back in the village."

Myers is gone, Mark is in charge of Fang, and I have no commitments. If I'm going to be seeing a man, a prominent man in our little village, it might be better to do it outside the microcosm. But it will take me forever in the traffic. And his timing is maddeningly awkward and beyond bad, but… *Oh, what the hell!*

"Sure. I can do that. Where do you want to meet?"

"There's a new place in Dilworth, a little wine bar called Twisted Vines over off of Woodlawn, near the movie theater."

"Okay… I know where the theater is."

"Would you like to try it out with me? I've never been, but it looks kind of funky and fun."

Funky and fun…am I that? "Yeah, that sounds nice."

"How long before you could get there?"

"I think in about—thirty minutes if the traffic isn't too bad."

"It won't be. Everyone in Charlotte is on vacation."

"Everyone except us."

"Except us. Okay. I'll see you then."

"Bye."

"Bye, Susannah."

I sit for a moment trying to compose myself. A date? Me? I can't believe I am swooning! This is ridiculous! I shake my head, wondering how I look. Chase hasn't been on a first date since 1988. That is so cute! And I haven't been on one since 2003, since my coffee shop rendezvous with Stan. Mathematically, all indications are that I should have the upper hand, but I certainly don't feel like I do! Asking me out might have been a lot harder for him to do than I think, so maybe I should feel flattered. I feel something, that's for sure! Whoa! I exhale again, long and slow, glad I acted on a whim and put on my pink and burgundy print dress this morning. I was in a good mood when I got up. Thinking I should get on the road, I check my makeup and hair in the mirror on the back of the door where I hang my lab coat. There isn't time to change anything, except apply a little Very Berry, so my appearance will have to do. Maybe this is a test to see how good I look at the end of the day, or to see how spontaneous I can be. That's ridiculous. I shouldn't over-think it. Whatever it is, I check my watch while dashing out of the office, calling my goodbyes to Lisa and Rosetta, who regard me as if I am a racehorse charging out of the gate, since I normally hang around and lollygag, especially after a fun day like today.

"Have a good evening! See you tomorrow," I call to avoid suspicion that something odd is up. Well, something odd is definitely up, and I begin to feel a little bit sick to my stomach. This is all so new to me. I shouldn't be nervous. Chase is nice and easy to talk to. I can have a glass of wine with him and then slink off to my own house. An hour of courage is all I need. Just sixty minutes, I think, checking my hair again in the rearview mirror before backing out of my parking spot.

Unless he suggests that we have dinner afterward. *Oh, God!*

I turn up the radio loud to calm my nerves. The Zac Brown Band is playing and there's a great fiddle part in this song. Chase likes country music like Myers does, so I blast it, wondering why Myers hasn't checked in with me yet. I got a call from him around seven-thirty last night, letting me know he and Tim had arrived safely and had finished their dinner. I could call him and try to make contact, but I don't think I want him to know what I'm doing. He'd probably freak out that I'm meeting the detective who's looking for Casey.

Chase was right. The traffic is surprisingly sparse for this time of the evening, and I have made it to the Dilworth neighborhood of Charlotte in just thirty minutes. I see the old movie theater and look around for Twisted Vines. First, the purple painted building catches my eye, and then the twisted grapevines that are painted over the door are apparent before I even make out the name on the sign. Outside, there are wrought iron tables and chairs with large tan umbrellas set up to ward off the July sun. Chase is already there, sitting in one of the chairs, and he stands when he sees my car drive up.

I set the parking brake and gather my skirt around me before exiting my car, trying for that charm school move where you swing your knees around together and set your feet on the ground, giving away no cheap shots for those inclined to look. I do it flawlessly, so my confidence swells. I have grace under fire. This is how it's done. It's like riding a bike. I can do this. I'm a grown woman going on an impromptu *date-not.*

I slip my purse over my arm and give him a smile as he waits for me to join him by the door. Chase really is a nice-looking guy. A vague recollection of a conversation with Patti reminds me that he's ex-military, like lots of cops are, but he doesn't have that macho swag that I dislike. I remember her saying he was in special operations. She was proud of him. I need to push thoughts of her away for now, or this encounter could become uncomfortable.

"Hi," I say.

"Hey," he smiles.

We'll go in and look over their wine menu and listen to the descriptions before we choose. Something red, I think, and it's then, when I'm almost at Chase's side, that my toe catches an uneven stone from the sidewalk and down I go. I feel myself falling, as if I have one hundred feet to go, but there is nothing I can do to save myself. Oh, no! I feel his hand grab my elbow, but even as quickly as he's reacted, it's too late. My knee makes a disgusting splat as it hits the sidewalk.

"Oh!" I pop back up, hoping no one saw my awkward *faux-pas*.

"Oh!" he says, righting me in one swoop. "Are you okay?"

"Yes. I'm fine. I think I've skinned my knee, but I'm sure I'll live."

Chase helps me to the nearest table and I sit down, feeling stupid. He hands me my purse, which I've dropped in the process.

"That looks painful," he says, down on one knee, examining mine, and producing a clean handkerchief from his pocket. I'm touched. Who carries a handkerchief anymore? I couldn't possibly put it on my bloody knee. A waiter is there in a moment with a wet paper towel for my wound, and both of us thank him.

"Oh, here." Chase applies the cool compress to my knee. I'm sure he is an excellent father.

"Thanks. You don't have to—I've got it. Thanks. That was embarrassing."

"No one saw...well, except our waiter. Don't worry."

The waiter continues the chivalrous behavior. "Stay right here, ma'am, and I'll bring out some menus if you'd like. I can go over the wine selections with you out here, unless you'd like to go inside. I have just the thing to make you feel better," he says, grinning and rubbing his hands together.

Chase sits in the chair next to me. We look at our waiter with questions on our faces.

He shrugs and extends his hands, "Wine!"

"Great. We'll just sit here for a minute," Chase says as our new friend disappears into the place in search of our menus.

"Is this all right?"

"It's perfect. I'm fine," I say, hoping he's not going to make a production of my injury. At least nobody laughed. It's a nice evening and we have a good table, right across the street from the old theater, where people are coming and going.

"Look, we can people-watch," he says, making me think that pastime has a different meaning for him, being a detective.

"When was the last time you fell down?" I ask.

"I couldn't tell you," he says, shaking his head.

"Remember falling down when you were a little kid? You just bounced right back up and went on your way like it was no big deal."

"Well…you didn't cry. I'm impressed. I always cried."

Imagining Chase crying makes me laugh as our waiter returns with menus and launches into his well-rehearsed narrative of all the delights that await us. As I'd hoped, Chase prefers red wine, so we order an alternative blend from California with an interesting name that promises to taste like chocolate-covered cherries with a currant finish. Chase shrugs and gives me a smirk. I'm no connoisseur, and apparently, neither is he, but it's fun to pretend.

"So what did you end up doing yesterday?" he asks, putting me even further at ease.

I prop my foot on the chair on the other side of me, and I settle the paper towel in place on my knee.

"Oh, all kinds of exciting stuff. I cleaned my house, except for Myers's room. I'm afraid to go in there!"

He laughs. "You won't catch me in Ryan's room either."

I twirl a curl around my finger while he watches. "And then I did some cooking. I made some squash casseroles from the squash out of my father's garden. I froze one for Mrs. Miller, took one over to my parents, and ate some of the one I kept." Chase nods, reflecting on Mrs. Miller, approving of the casserole reference. "Then I played the piano—show tunes, mostly. And then after dark when the fireworks started, I went on my run around the park and through the neighborhood!"

"Huh! I've never run during the fireworks."

"Me neither. It was really cool! It was a great way to see them," I say.

"You should have stopped in for watermelon, now that you know the way," he says, making me realize that he spent the evening alone like I did. Our waiter arrives to pour our wine, and he chats us up about what we are about to experience, neatly saving me from having to reply.

The waiter leaves and Chase picks up his glass. "What shall we drink to?"

I think for a minute. "How about to the Casserole Queen?"

"Mrs. Miller? Great idea," he says, lifting his glass to meet mine. "To the Casserole Queen."

We take a sip. The wine is all it was promised to be, and we grin, as if so surprised.

"Speaking of the Casserole Queen, I talked to Mark today," I say, making Chase look interested.

"How's his mom?"

"Her doctor did surgery last night. She suffered an anterior left temporal lobe hemorrhage, which he was able to repair, and she got through it pretty well."

Chase looks lost. "Can you explain that in laymen's terms?"

"There was a bleed in the part of her brain that controls her speech output. She can understand what's being said, but she can't get her words out. The left temporal lobe is the speech center." He watches me gesture to the area over my left ear to illustrate.

"Oh."

"He said she was starting to get some of her speech back, but it's still hard to hear her, and her words are slurred, what little she's able to get out. There's some weakness on her right side, but they won't really know much more until they try to assess her for walking and occupational skills like eating and using her hands to wash and dress herself, that kind of thing."

Chase looks stunned. "I guess that's good. How long will she be like that?"

"It's hard to say just yet. She could improve very quickly over the first few days and weeks. 'If and when' is how the doctors usually phrase a patient's prognosis because she has other factors like her age and possibly other health issues that could impact her progress. Hopefully, she can improve to the point where she can enter rehabilitation and get the therapy she'll need to progress even further. It's a day-by-day thing for her right now."

Chase studies a point on the sidewalk as he lets this information sink in. "Wow," he says, looking at me. "How long are Mark and Brenda planning to stay here?"

"They're going to stay in her house over the weekend and see how it goes. I told them that whenever they go back to Columbia, I'll take Fang to my house and take care of him."

Chase grins. "Fang, the little hero."

"I know. Maybe he saved her life…like in the old *Lassie* shows."

He laughs and takes another sip of his wine.

"Do you have a pet?"

"No," he says. "I grew up on a farm in Alabama with all kinds of animals, so it seems strange not to have one anymore. We had dogs when the kids were little. Olivia thinks I should get a dog. I'm never home, though, so it would seem unfair."

His story, so like mine, makes me smile. "Same here." I lift my glass to sip my wine as well, and since I'm left-handed, he seems to take it into account, the way people do sometimes. I also notice him glancing at my ring.

"You still wear your ring," he says. I don't know why his directness surprises me.

"Yes. So do you."

He leans forward, running the tip of his finger around the glass's rim. "I guess I always thought I'd wear it. That's one of the reasons I wanted to talk to you. You haven't seemed to have moved on either."

A strange sense of disappointment flows over me. I didn't think he wanted to meet me just to talk about our deceased spouses, but I'm so obviously connected to Stan, and he apparently is to Patti. So that was what this date-not was all about. He didn't want to go out with me at all. *This is a therapy session.* The let-down must show in my face.

"I'm sorry…I just thought—I mean, I wondered how you're handling yourself after so many years. I can't…seem to get past it." He shrugs, possibly unwilling to put anymore on the line due to whatever he saw on my face, so I immediately shift gears. I can play counselor. I do it every day.

"No. I certainly understand where you're coming from. I obviously have the same problem," I say, twisting the band on my finger. "It's been three years, and I still have Stan's clothes in the closet. And for what it's worth, I don't think it's a bad thing. You move on when you're ready. And maybe you're not ready. That's not a bad thing either."

He looks relieved that I'm willing to discuss my own struggle.

"You know, it's weird, but it's like I can still hear Patti talking to me. It's like she's still here." He shakes his head. "I don't know if it'll ever stop. Did that ever happen to you?"

My eyes widen and I look away. I sip my wine to compose myself. "Yes. It used to happen to me all the time. I think it does stop, gradually. But it takes time. Stan always talked to me too, until just very recently. And I don't know what that's about," I say, lifting a hand in concession. *I wear his bathrobe all the time,* I want to say. Chase doesn't seem emotional, thank goodness, so I continue. "I feel…deserted in a way. Here,

Myers is going to leave in a month and I'm going to be alone. I thought now would be the time that Stan would step up his game…."

"Is there a place it happens? Where you hear him?"

"It used to be anywhere, everywhere, but mostly on our front porch swing. When he was alive, we used to sit there for hours, talking, especially at night when Myers was asleep, or in the mornings on weekends, when we'd sit out there, drinking our coffee. And just talk. How about for you?"

"Lots of places. Home. There's a park bench in Pacific Grove, my sister's town I was telling you about. Patti's especially present there. The bench is right on the cliff, under a big cypress tree, overlooking the ocean. The view is incredible, and we'd sit there, talking about the kids, our hopes and dreams. You couldn't help but dream out there, it's so beautiful! I'm going back in a couple of weeks for vacation and then to fly home with Olivia. I'll be interested to see if I still have that same experience."

"Do you want to? I mean, do you want Patti to continue talking to you?"

He looks into my eyes and studies me. "I don't know. I think it would be easier for me if I could move on. Most people take about a year and they're ready, but…." He looks down at his glass.

"I know. That's what I thought, and here I am…." I shrug. "But now…I think Stan's trying to cut me off," I laugh, tracing my finger around the base of my goblet.

He smiles. "Well, I didn't mean to be such a downer. It's just nice to talk to someone who really understands. You know? And just talk about the elephant in the room instead of agonizing about it all by myself. Other people forget after a couple of years go by, you know? But sometimes I still feel the need to talk about her…."

"I know. It's because you really loved her. I loved Stan so much I wasn't willing to let him go, either."

He stares at the table and so do I. I have just used the past tense in reference to my feelings for Stan. I don't normally do that.

"And by the way, I want you to know that I really appreciate everything you did for Patti. She said you were great. I couldn't tell you that when I was losing her."

The sudden and unexpected emotion in his voice breaks my heart. "I wish I could have done more."

"You couldn't have. You *couldn't have*," he says again, perhaps understanding how inadequate I felt about Patti's case.

I don't know what to say. He watches me.

"What happened to Stan?"

God, his questions are so invasive! But why am I surprised? Talking to Chase requires more and more soul-baring each time we are together. The cathartic feelings he brings out in me teeter on the border of both pleasure and pain, making me struggle to look introspectively. This must be what facing addiction feels like. I haven't talked about Stan's death in years. Telling the story requires a deep breath so I can get my bearings.

"He was an emergency room doc. Always busy, always stressed out. He worked more than he should have, but it was the nature of his job, you know? He didn't bring the stress home, though. Or at least, I didn't think he did. He put his entire being into his work when he was there. But he was one to live in the moment. We lost him suddenly and ironically. One night he was on duty and he told one of the nurses he felt funny and excused himself. The staff was looking for him everywhere and no one could find him. He'd gone into the men's room, locked himself in a stall, and had a massive heart attack. And that was it."

"Oh, my God!" He wonders for a moment. "How does that happen to a doctor?"

I shrug. "Doctors are the worst patients. It was the stress of the job. I thought he was in good shape, but he didn't have time to exercise regularly, and he didn't eat right a lot of the time. And worse than that, we didn't know all of his family history. If his father had any kind of heart disease, we didn't know. His dad deserted his mother when Stan was very young, so there was no way to know. There was no indication, no reason ever to expect anything like that would happen."

Chase gazes at me with compassion. "And you never had the chance to say goodbye."

I shake my head and turn my face away. I don't want him to see that I still grieve like this. Looking at the theater, the large numbers of people pouring out catch my eye; I think about Chase's remark about people-watching. I want him to watch those people across the street and not me.

"No, I didn't." I take a large sip of my wine. Maybe Stan is through with me, but I don't think I'm finished with him. Meeting Chase tonight was a bad idea.

"I'm so sorry, Susannah." He takes a deep breath. "Let's change the subject, okay? I didn't really ask you here to talk about all of this. I really did just want to get to know you better."

But you're not ready either, I think to myself. Our wedding rings tell us two things. *I can't have you, and you can't have me.* The wine's effects are starting to work on me. There's a little pressure on my eyes, and my lips are getting slightly numb. I must be seeing things. Even strangers are starting to look familiar. I try to clear my head, focusing in on one of the boys across the street. He holds two tickets and hands one to the cute blonde who is wishing he'd hold her hand. Something about him is familiar—his posture, the haircut, the bright orange tennis shoes. Then he turns around and laughs at something the girl says. I swallow hard and set my glass on the table. Chase cocks his head and looks at me.

"Wait—what is *Tim* doing here?"

Chapter 13

SEARCH PARTY

"What is it, Susannah?"

I'm hurtled back into reality, forgetting our ghostly spouses, and my attention is glued to the young man across the street with the sun-kissed blond hair, who is about to disappear inside the movie theater with his matching girlfriend. I jar the table as I bolt out of my chair, the damp paper towel falling from my knee to the ground. Chase does his best to steady our wine bottle as I grab my purse and start to dash across the street.

"Hey! Tim!" I shout, halfway across the street, forcing an oncoming car to screech to a stop in my wake. Tim's form hesitates as he hears his name called. I call out again so he can locate the voice, and then he freezes like a scared rabbit when he sees me coming for him. I can hear Chase's footsteps behind me.

"Tim!"

"Oh! Hey. Dr. Brody," he says and I can see the lump of his Adam's apple rise and fall as he swallows hard. This time, the scared rabbit has been replaced by a deer-in-headlights, and his eyes dart around, the cute girl at his side completely forgotten.

"What are you doing here? I thought you were camping on Roan Mountain with Myers?" I demand, slinging my purse over my shoulder, barely noticing Chase, who looks ready to jump into the fray and pry me off of this kid if necessary. I guess I look as mad as I feel. My head is spinning as Tim struggles for words. He raises his hands in defense as all of us wait for him to speak.

"I—I-uh…Myers asked me not to say. He told me he had to go away for a few days and for me to lay low in Magnolia until Sunday. I—I didn't think anybody'd see me over here," he says, eyes darting around. His girlfriend's mouth is shaped in an O, and Chase looks at me to see what I'll say next.

"Great. So he's lied to me. Where is he, Tim? I'm calling your mother if you don't tell me."

"I—you—you can call her, but all I can tell you is I don't know where he is."

"Tim?" Chase's voice is charged with authority, and he whips his badge out of his jacket pocket. "I'm Detective Andrew Chase with the Fort Mill Police Department, Tim. If you know anything at all, you need to tell us. I'm investigating the disappearance of Casey French, and it would be in your best interest to cooperate fully," he says, staring Tim down with those intimidating eyes. He seems a foot taller when he does that, I notice with relief, hoping he'll get something out of Tim.

"I'm sorry, Detective, but I really don't know where he is. I was just tryin' to help him out. I guess he didn't tell me where he was going on purpose."

"Is he with Casey now?" Chase persists.

"Like I said, I don't know. He just said he had to take care of something and needed a reason to get out of town without a lot of questions."

Chase glances at me. *Myers is protecting Casey.*

I am on my cell phone to Myers, as Tim and the girl are looking around at the other people going into the theater. The phone rings and rings, but there is no answer, just his usual voicemail prompt. They listen while I leave a message. "Myers, call me. I'm standing here with Tim in Charlotte, so where are you?"

Chase turns back to Tim. "Do you know another way to get in touch with Myers?"

"No. Just his cell phone."

"Call him," says Chase, as I put my phone back in my purse. Tim pulls his phone out of his pocket and places the call but he, too, gets the voicemail prompt. He leaves a message for Myers to call him, then shrugs and looks at Chase. "When was the last time you spoke to Myers?" Chase asks.

"Probably...Wednesday. He asked me to stay out of sight in the village until Sunday. He said he was going to tell you that we were going camping and that I shouldn't be seen until I heard from him again, probably on Saturday or Sunday. But he hasn't called me," Tim says, looking shamefully at me.

"So, where have you been, Tim, once you got your orders from Myers?" Chase pokes, and I know immediately that he's trying to make Tim angry enough to rat out Myers. Making him look stupid in front of this girl could be useful.

"I came over here yesterday to visit Christina, and then I came back today..." *so he wouldn't be seen in Magnolia.*

Ah! Poor Christina has figured out that she's been played, it seems, judging by the pursed lips and hands stuffed in her back pockets. And here she thought sweet Tim was so infatuated with her that he couldn't stay away!

"So you've spent two days taking up this nice young lady's time, just so you could stay out of the spotlight?" Chase hammers home his point. Tim stares at the ground, while Christina rolls her eyes and watches the other people going into the theater. They're going to be late for their movie.

"That wasn't the only reason," Tim says irritably.

"Do you know where Casey French is?"

"No."

"I'll ask you again. Do you know where Myers Morgan is? If you're withholding information and either one of them gets hurt, it could be on you, Tim. Are you prepared for that responsibility?"

Wow. He's good.

Tim swallows again, hard this time. "No, sir. But like I said, I don't know where either one of them is."

Chase hands him one of his business cards. "Okay, Tim. If you think of anything else, you call me."

I have nothing further to add, so I flip my eyebrows at Tim and glance at Christina. "I *will* call your mother," I throw in, however ineffectively, as Chase and I leave them on the sidewalk. The anger that propels me across the street lifts me from any feeling in my feet. Now, completely sober, I reel on Chase because there is no one else.

"He lied to me. Myers lied. And it wasn't any little white lie either; it was a premeditated act of pure *perjury!*"

"Whoa, take it easy," he says, laying a hand on my shoulder. "Myers is protecting Casey."

"Then she must be in trouble. How can I not know what's going on?" I shout, frustrated with myself for missing the clues. Chase picks up on my thoughts.

"What are you missing, Susannah? What's Myers been saying or doing that strikes you as odd?" he asks as we stand in the parking lot at my car. I can see the half bottle of wine and our empty glasses at our table still.

"There have been several things. He hasn't been himself since he got back from music camp. I thought he was just distancing himself from me because he's sick of being at home. He wasn't playing his violin. He acts like I've been crowding him...and then he's been holed up in his room, saying he's tired and doesn't feel well. None of that is like him. And then he changed his ringtone and changed it back…. No! Oh, God! Of course!"

"What?"

"You know, when you said Casey might have used a burner phone to avoid leaving a trail? I think he might be using one too. I heard two different rings. He has two phones."

"That's how he's communicating with her."

"Why the hell can't she just call in? What could she have done that would be so bad that she couldn't tell Maggie? Why can't he tell me what's going on? And where *are* they?"

"Okay," Chase says, his voice lowering so I will calm down. People are starting to stare at us. "Listen, I don't have any warrants on Myers, but you can search around on your own and see what you can come up with."

"You mean, like going through his Facebook account?"

He shrugs. "Legally, I can't advise you to do that, but lots of parents do it. If you were to discover something by happenstance, it might help you rest easier…until you hear from him, at least. And you *will* hear from him. From what y'all have said about Casey and Myers, they don't strike me as kids who've gone off the deep end."

I gaze at him a moment. He is trying to help.

He continues. "Listen, I'll stop by the station and check in with the hospitals and some places to rule out that he's fallen in harm's way."

"Do you mind? It's getting late and you haven't eaten."

"Neither have you. I can grab a sandwich." I look at him warily. "Look, it's what I do, okay?"

Our waiter has appeared beside us with the corked wine bottle in a black paper wrapper. "Don't leave without your other half," he says, wondering what's going on.

"Thanks, man," Chase says, taking the twisted paper bag, and fishing out a couple of bills from his money clip. Suddenly, watching Chase pay the waiter, I feel tired, realizing I have nothing to go on in the search for my son. Knowing I'll be up half the night prowling through Myers's virtual life, I feel the need to fade away, crawl into my pajamas, and be left alone.

"Thank you for a nice evening," I say, not really knowing what to call our encounter, or why I really feel the need to thank him. He did buy me a glass of wine.

Chase looks at me as if he understands the night has been a grave disappointment.

"I'll call you later and let you know what I find out. Call me, too, if you hear from him, okay?"

"Thank you. I will," I say, pointing the remote at my car to unlock the door. He holds the door for me and tells me to take care again as I back out of my parking spot.

An empty feeling fills the car as I take my place in the queue at the stoplight. The sun is sinking, washing the sky with lavender dusk. I can't get home soon enough. The dreaded necessary task nags at me all the way home, but it is not until I walk through the kitchen door that I can act on it.

I toss my purse onto the desk and place my keys in the blue pottery bowl next to it, reminding myself to check the mail later. Sighing, I start to fill a glass of water at the sink, and then I check my box of coffee filters in the cupboard to see whether I have a message. It is wishful thinking, but there is nothing. I make my way into the living room and sink down onto the couch, curling my feet under me, and address the screen on my cell phone. I can never call Kent without remembering how he betrayed my trust on one of these simple devices. But he needs to know that Myers is missing.

Kent's phone rings four times before he picks up. "Susannah? What's up?" he murmurs sleepily.

"Hi, Kent. Were you asleep?"

I hear him chuckle. "No."

"You haven't spoken to Myers in the past couple of days have you?"

"No, why?"

"He's gone off and I don't know where he is. He told me on Wednesday that he was going backpacking up on the Appalachian Trail near Roan Mountain with Tim—but I just ran into Tim tonight in Charlotte. He said Myers told him to lie low until he calls or returns on Sunday."

"What? That doesn't sound like Myers at all."

"I know. He lied to me."

"What's going on?" he asks in a distinct accusatory tone. I ignore it as usual.

"Casey French has been missing for several days. I think he's gone to find her, or be with her, but of course, he hasn't told me anything about it."

"You need to call the police."

"The police are already investigating. The detective on her case is also working on Myers's disappearance as we speak."

There is silence at first and then muted rustling and whispering on his end, as if he is talking to someone else.

He clears his throat. "What do you need me to do?"

"I don't know. I just felt that you needed to be informed. I also wanted to check with you to see if he'd contacted you."

"No. No, we haven't talked since the camping trip."

"Really?"

"Really. When is he leaving for college?"

"We're going up to Nashville on August tenth."

"Just a month…"

"Yeah."

"Well, let me know if you hear from him. I'd like to see him before he takes off."

I inhale and sigh. "Okay. You call me if he calls you, too, okay?"

"Sure. He'll turn up, Susannah. But I'll call you if I hear from him."

"Okay, bye." I press the end button and hold the phone to my chin. Was he with Jen? If he had been with her, wouldn't he have put her on the phone, or mentioned that I was calling? I shake my head. It's too much to try and conjecture about any of the men I know right now, even the dead ones.

"Ahh!" I shout, pushing myself off the couch. I walk back to my bedroom and strip off my dress. I think about my pajamas and realize my favorite pair is in the dirty clothes. I didn't get to all the laundry yesterday when I left to see my parents. Finding myself staring at Stan's closet door, I open it and look again at his clothes. I try to imagine Stan being here and what he'd do to help. Regardless of the futility of the situation, he was good at making me feel better. The plaid robe somehow makes its way into my hands and I slip inside it, tying it around me, liking the way it engulfs me. "Please, talk to me…" I mutter, knowing I'll get nothing.

I should eat, I think, walking back into the kitchen in the twilight, but I have no appetite. Instead, I turn on the burner under my tea kettle, then find a mug and a tea bag from the cupboard. I think about Myers's room, wondering what secrets might be hidden there in the mess if I just allow myself to invade his privacy. As angry as I am right now, I will have no problem doing that!

Minutes later, I am carrying my orange tea into his room, flipping on the light and looking around. It smells like a gym in here, I think, wrinkling my nose and sallying forth amidst the clothes that lie in piles on the floor and on his chair. Clearing a place to set my tea mug on his desk, I rummage through his papers, looking for notes, college packets, old camp materials, and music he's writing. I study the sheet music for a moment, wondering about playing his melodies on the piano later. His new laptop sits closed on his desk. If he were trying to cover his tracks, he should have taken this with him. He also must know exactly where he's going, not to leave notes.

I open the computer and power it up. I don't have his password, so I look through the college packet to see whether I'm lucky like Maggie was. I find his login information with his new college email address and password that I write down for future reference. I type in the password *Restless13!* on the login screen and wait. It's the name of one of his favorite songs from the early '90s that was recorded by The New Nashville Cats, a band that included Vince Gill, Steve Wariner, Ricky Skaggs, and Myers's idol, Mark O'Connor. The screen comes to life and icons appear. I click on the Facebook icon and try the password again. This has to be it…but I don't get in. I'm deflated that it is not the one I need to see inside his life. I can use my own login to access the site, but I won't be able to read his messages. I try other combinations, thinking back on his previous life to try to imagine what he'd use. The password is bound to have something to do with music, so I try various combinations, knowing the numerical part is what's going to stump me. *Fiddlenbow2013* gets me nowhere, *play4you64* uses his birthday, but I'm still not in. I could do this all night, and after a certain amount of attempts, the site no longer lets me try.

I log in under my own account and sip my tea, as I search for his name and his page pops up. Like Maggie, I'm also shocked that Myers has almost a thousand friends. I scroll carefully down through his posts. He has posted nothing since the beginning of music camp. I click on his friends and scroll through to see which ones I know and which ones I don't. I quickly conclude that taking notes is in order, so I find a piece of paper and begin writing down names. He and Casey must know mutual friends who live out of town. That information should help, but also, like Maggie, I realize this will be a daunting task, not knowing his password.

There are so many girls on this site! I am stunned at the number of lovely faces that stare back at me from the screen. And all of them pose with a hand on one of their hips! I've heard this chicken-wing pose makes ones arms look more slender, so I guess if I have heard it, then they certainly have too! I'll have to try it myself.

At least thirty minutes have elapsed and my neck is getting stiff when my phone rings. It is Chase. My heart plummets.

"Hi. Did you find out anything?" I ask, a hint of dread in my voice.

"No. You'll be relieved to know I didn't find Myers in any of the local emergency rooms, or in any of the police reports. What are you doing?"

"I'm looking at his Facebook page, but I couldn't hack his password. I'd love to know if he and Casey have any friends in common."

"You know her password…" he says. I must be getting tired; I'd forgotten.

"Yeah, I guess I could look through hers and cross-reference. I can look at her messages and see if there are any cryptic ones between Myers and her."

"Well, I'm almost home," he says, but I am distracted by familiar dark eyes that stare back at me on the screen. I check the name and click on it, showing me where the girl lives. Why didn't I think of this before?

"Oh—wait! Holy crap! I think I found something!"

"What?"

"My niece, Sloan, Myers's cousin—is showing up as one of his friends. At least I think this is her. I haven't seen her in a while. She's using another name, though. *Velveeta Cheeser.*"

"What? Weird."

"Tell me about it. She's always had kind of a sick sense of humor. She lives in New York, and it just hit me that Casey has met her before."

"Are they close? Myers and...*Velveeta*?"

"No, not really."

"Do you have her number?"

"No, but I can call my sister and get it."

"I'm pulling up in front of your house right now." He sounds excited. This is what detectives live for, apparently. I feel more than a little tingle myself, sharing in it with him.

"You're a junkie for this kind of thing, aren't you?"

"Damn right." He disconnects, and in the time it takes me to grab the laptop and my tea and to make my way carefully down the stairs without spilling it, I hear the doorbell ring. *Dang it!* I'm still in Stan's robe!

What the hell? I set everything down on the kitchen table and open the door. It's dark by now, and here I stand in my nightclothes. Chase doesn't look twice at me in my bare feet and man-sized robe. I haven't even gotten around to bandaging my skinned knee. When I hold the door for him to come in, he homes right in on the laptop screen on the table.

"Show me what you've got."

"Right here."

"This is your niece?" I understand his surprise that there is no family resemblance and the heavy, Gothic-looking young woman in professional makeup and facial piercings looks nothing like me, except for the coloring, possibly.

"No way I'd have connected the two of you," he says, sitting and scrolling over her information.

"Well, my sister and I are both adopted and her husband was very dark and...kind of swarthy." He nods, taking it in. If he only knew about Kent and Jen....

"Huh. Is she an actress?"

"No, she's a full-figure model."

"Okay, explains that name…it is kind of sick. So, how does Casey know her?"

"Sloan was here last spring and happened to go to Casey's school play—*South Pacific*—with Myers, so I know they met. That's all I know."

"Okay, let's switch over to Casey's page and see if there are any messages," he says, clicking away on the keyboard until Casey's face pops up. He types in Sloan's alias and then clicks on the message tab. A conversation appears and we both take a breath. "It looks like they talked back in April. Look at this," he says, pointing at the screen. "The last thing Velveeta says is, 'If you want to come up, you can crash at my place.'"

"I'm calling Jen right now," I say, placing my call on my phone and waiting for it to ring. It rings several times and Jen's voice message comes on, instructing me to leave a message. "Jen, it's Susannah. Call me as soon as you get this. I need Sloan's phone number. And by the way, Myers and his friend Casey are missing and I think Sloan might have something to do with it."

"That ought to get her to call you back." I disregard Chase's comment and try Jen's home phone, which rings four times and sends me to her voicemail. I leave the same message, this time, imitating that formidable voice Chase uses when intimidating his victims.

"Hmm," I say, looking back at the screen, wondering why she didn't call me if she's with Kent. Okay, so if she isn't with Kent, why did he sound like he was in bed with someone at nine o'clock at night? And if he wasn't with Jen, then who was he with?

"Have you checked Myers's bank account balance?"

"No, but he has plenty of money he could get his hands on…" I say, watching Chase scroll up and down the page. From my vantage point, I can observe Chase without him noticing me. At the base of his neatly razored sideburn, I can barely make out the end of the tiny scar I made from his surgical procedure years ago. He takes a quick breath through his teeth, making me aware that he does this when he gets an idea.

"Has Casey ever been to New York?"

"Yeah. Maggie and Ed took her one time. They went to some shows and the symphony."

Chase has left the Facebook screen and begins a Google search for something.

"I should call Maggie…. What are you looking for?"

"Okay, let's say that Casey wants to go to New York and audition for some shows. I'm searching for Broadway auditions this week."

"Of course. That's brilliant!"

"I was thinking when you said that Sloan is a full-figure model, maybe Casey identifies with her. And she's just had the leading role in *Hairspray*, so maybe she's decided to buck her parents' wishes and go for the big cheese—in the Big Apple."

"Do you know what it's about? Have you ever seen *Hairspray*?"

"What do you think I was doing last night when I was *all by myself*?"

I chuckle, imagining him at home alone on July Fourth, eating watermelon and watching the musical about a pleasingly-plump wannabe dancer, who breaks racial barriers—and weight barriers, too, in the process. "Did you watch *South Pacific* too?"

"Yes, ma'am, I did."

His search lists several auditions in New York this week. He takes out a small notepad from his jacket pocket and starts writing.

"This one," I say, pointing out a link to an audition for a musical in New York that's currently running. Chase clicks on the link and writes down the name of the play and the contact information.

"What can you do with this? New York's not exactly your jurisdiction."

"I have friends all over, my dear. And there's a favor or two I can call up."

He scrolls down to the next link and we both gasp. "Now that title's ironic."

"Yes it is. *Plus Size.*"

Chapter 14

TIMING IS EVERYTHING

Why is it when there is an emergency, no one answers her damn phone? I can't reach Maggie either, making me wonder what great movie I must be missing. The only times I silence my phone are when I'm at work, at church, in one of Myers's performances, and at the movies. A movie is my best guess for all of these people on a Friday night. I grumble, looking at Velveeta's image, and that cheeky, in-your-face grin on someone who's having the last laugh on you. My sister has created a monster. And poor Casey French has been taken in by her evil charms! If any of this is true at all, it makes me want to vomit.

I can't let myself get wound up like this or I will never sleep; however, I do have just the medication for that. It's eleven-thirty and too late to call anybody. Thinking I'll raid the medicine cabinet and get on with trying to sleep, I second-guess myself, wondering whether I'd hear my phone ring if Myers were to call in. My hips and back ache from sitting at the computer screen, so I force myself to give it up, stand, and stretch my arms high over my head and hinge forward to touch my toes. I reach up in sun salutation fashion and power off the laptop. I'll plug in my phone charger by my bed, read for a while, and pray for sleep.

Chase is a prince the way he dashed off gallantly with another idea to pursue, evidently something he couldn't do in my kitchen, and I have to admit, I was glad to see him go. Even though his very presence is reassuring, I was getting really tired and restless. Also, I felt odd standing over his shoulder in nothing but Stan's robe, although Chase never looked at me funny, or said a word about it. I guess that is the detective in him. *Never let them see what you're thinking.* Something inside me, a tiny little unfamiliar feminine voice, however, was crying out to be noticed, and I squashed her…at least twice. I wonder whether he heard her speaking.

Apparently not.

When my alarm goes off at six o'clock, I slap my hand over the snooze button. My other hand goes over my forehead, and I stretch, realizing that it's Saturday and there is no reason to hurry. But then there is. I sit up immediately, trying to get my bearings, push my hair away from my face, and reach for my phone. Pressing buttons frantically, I soon discover there were no calls or messages in the middle of the night from Myers. *Damn it!*

I am wide-awake now. Heaving myself out of bed, I throw on Stan's robe and make my way into the kitchen where the coffeepot awaits my attention. Going through my morning ritual of brewing the coffee and opening my laptop to check the morning news, I think about Mrs. Miller in the hospital, realizing that her paper is probably lying on the sidewalk next door, but then I remember that Mark and Brenda are there to take care of it. I will call them later to check on her…and Fang, my new friend.

Sipping my coffee, I return to my bedroom and slip into fresh running shorts and a blue tank top, grab my shoes and socks, and head for the front porch. I sit in the swing and drink my coffee, acutely aware that one more person in my life has departed, though not for good, I hope. Still, the thought is unsettling, and as I move to the floor to stretch out my legs, I try not to take it personally. Perhaps my existence is not as important to some people as I had imagined. It's a humbling thought, but I am determined not to let it get me down. I could sit inside moping and eating junk food all day, but that would do me no good. I need endorphins. A morning run is just the thing to erode the funk that looms in front of me, so I smear on my sunscreen, slap on my cap, and off I go.

I run past the park, under the soft gray canopy of the maple trees, enjoying the heavy moist scents of the morning, the grass and flowers and freshly turned soil. Someone is gardening. It's amazing what you can train yourself to discover through the senses. I smell water from a hose, and hear the tick-tick-tick of a neighbor's sprinkler as I jog by. An elderly man with a potbelly walks his dog, a cute little brown and black creature whose species probably ends with "poo." I should get a dog, I think, realizing that I really am alone. A lap dog maybe, that wouldn't shed and could sleep in the curve of my knees at night and would sing me to sleep with soft snoring.

I turn left, instead of my usual right, and find myself running past Chase's house, wondering whether he's up. His empty planters by the front door bother me. They should be spilling over with pretty flowers. A lamp burns in a front window, odd for this time of the morning. Maybe he was up late, investigating or whatever it is that he does. I never go this way, and I wonder what compels me this morning. An uncomfortable feeling overtakes me; I shouldn't be here. I'm intruding on Chase, and Patti, and Olivia. He is still so involved with his family.

Our *date-not* certainly did not go as I'd expected. What *did* I expect? So uncharacteristically of me, I let my guard down. I let myself go off the deep end, like some pathetic high-schooler, waiting for that one special guy to open up her world. Stupid. I'm old enough and smart enough to know better. I felt a strange kinship with that cute little Christina who was with Tim last night. He burst the first of her many bubbles, too. So did I allow Chase to get close enough to burst my bubble? What was I thinking? I knew better than to expect a man like Stan to come along and sweep me off my feet again. He was one of a kind. Past tense. Chase is one of those kinds of guys, but he is obviously just *not that into me*. I'm even thinking in clichés. This nonsense has to stop. Reality, like medicine, is cut and dry. It is all that matters. That, and wishing my dead husband would talk to me again. I really do need therapy.

Thirty minutes later, I am back on my porch, watering my ferns and potted red geraniums, sitting on the swing, drinking a glass of water, and cooling down enough to take my shower. I check my phone again, but still no calls, and no messages. At least my sister could return my frantic cry for help! I hope she'll call me before running to Mom and Dad about it first. They certainly don't need to be bothered with all this excitement until we know what is going on. The sins of omission…lies, too, I recall. I was a master at keeping things from my parents as an adolescent, just like I'm doing now. It's the same way my son is treating me. Stan the Man would be pissed at him too!

Freshly showered and clothed, I sit at Myers's laptop again while I eat my English muffin and banana with my second cup of coffee. I go to the Facebook login page. There has to be a password I can figure out. When did he start using Facebook? I remembered Stan, sitting with Casey and Myers in the kitchen, looking at the first Facebook posts he'd made, and thinking it was a real turning point in Myers's life, getting into social media. Boy, was I right! Still, it was a time in his life when he was so close to Stan, and I thought it was duly significant that Stan was there, being allowed to watch the two kids interact on the Internet. Myers was fifteen and Stan was fifty-one. Even Casey was infatuated with Stan, his hot doctor persona, and his easy accent. She was the first of us to call him "Stan the Man." I sit up quickly and type in a password: *Stantheman1551*. Nothing. I try again, *1551Stantheman*. Nothing. *Stantheman5115*. Nothing. And then I recall the way he and Myers would count out a measure before starting to play a piece together. *1234Stantheman*.

Bingo! I'm in.

It takes no time to find Velveeta Cheeser on the screen so I hit *messages* and hold my breath. There aren't many messages there, and most of them don't seem to mean anything—except the last one, dated Tuesday at 1:50 p.m. *Package arrived!*

"Holy shit!" I mutter under my breath and reach for my phone. Who should I call first? Jen. I have to get Sloan's phone number to see whether I'm really on the right track! My hands are shaking as I place the call.

She answers after two rings.

"Hi, Susannah." Her voice sounds groggy, as if I've woken her. It's nine o'clock for goodness sake!

"Jen! Didn't you get my message last night?"

"Yeah, I saw you'd called, but it was late." Now she sounds irritable. "I went to a movie with some friends and we stopped off for drinks afterwards. I guess my phone was still on vibrate."

"Did you listen to the message? Myers is missing, and so is Casey French. I think they're in New York with Sloan. I need her number. And her address," I add, thinking Chase will need it.

"Wait, whoa, hold the phone…" she says, and I can imagine her, trying to collect herself in the throes of her hangover.

"You weren't with Kent last night?"

"No. He was working," she says, and I detect that familiar distinct bitterness, the same tone I used to use when discussing Kent's work habits, but I decide to drop the topic like a hot rock.

"Did you know that Sloan's name on Facebook is Velveeta Cheeser?"

"Oh, my God, Susannah! Are you *stalking* her?"

"I'm trying to find our children. Seriously? *Velveeta?*"

"You know her sense of humor. Do you want me to call her?"

"No. I want her number. When's the last time you've talked to her?"

"I don't know…a couple of months? I'll call her and see what's up."

A couple of months? I'd kill Myers if he went that long without a word, but then, that's Jen and Sloan's dysfunctional relationship. Still, this whole crazy situation is making me even more impatient. "I'm going to call her myself. Do you have her number?"

"Wait a minute. I'll call you back. I don't know how to get her number from my phone contacts without hanging up on you." She disconnects and I roll my eyes, tapping my fingers on the table nervously. In a moment, she calls me back. I write down the phone number and address, thank Jen, and hang up. I call the number and there is no answer. Great.

Chase is next.

"What's up, Detective?" he asks into the phone, making me laugh. My name must be in his contacts for him to know it's me. His voice sounds tired.

"Good morning. I have a phone number and address for Velveeta. I called the phone number and guess what?"

"No answer."

"You got it."

"Damn! That's par for the course. Half of the people I've been calling on this case don't answer their phones. That Spencer Wilson kid never picked up, and when I went by the house, the neighbors said they're out of the country on vacation, like everybody else in the world." He's followed up on all the leads.

"That's convenient."

"Never work a case in July."

"I'll keep that in mind. I cracked Myers's password and got into his messages with Velveeta. There was one on Tuesday afternoon at 1:50 that said, 'Package arrived!'"

"Well, aren't you the little sleuth! What was the magic word?"

"1-2-3-4 Stan the man."

There's a silence, and then he says, "They must have been close."

"Yes, they were. So what are you working on?"

"I was up most of the night looking over the train station passenger manifests. I've got a friend, an old army buddy, who's a private investigator in New York following up a lead I caught, so I'm waiting on him to get back to me." He sounds evasive. *Is he protecting me?*

"Do you have him checking the hospitals?"

"Yeah, actually. That, and the police reports, and a couple of other things. I'll give him this address to check out as well. As soon as I know anything definitive, I'll call you and Maggie. Have you talked to her this morning?"

"No, but she's my next call."

"Okay. Good. I hope she answers."

"Me too."

"I'll talk to you later."

"Okay. Bye." I wait just a minute to let all this new information register. Chase was up most of the night looking for my son and his best friend. I know it's his job, but it makes me feel good.

Maggie answers on the fourth ring. "Hey!"

"Hey!" I reply, equally as glad to hear her voice. "How was the Fourth?" I ask, thinking I'll start her out slowly, even though my heart is still pounding. I know how stress needs gentle stroking.

"We had an absolute blast! I actually got a little sunburned, even though I used my sunscreen!"

I make scolding noises with my tongue. "Well, I'm glad you had fun."

"What did you do?"

"Well, first thing in the morning my neighbor had a stroke and had to go to the hospital...."

"Oh, no! Mrs. Miller?"

"Yeah. Her son and daughter-in-law came and I'm waiting to hear how she is. Then, I went by my parents' for a little while. They were still feeling too puny to watch the fireworks, so I ran while the show was going on. It was so cool!" I think it's best if I don't expound on my hospital adventure with Mrs. Miller and Chase, or the date-not. Maggie will get ideas.

"Well, that's different."

"I guess you haven't heard from Casey."

"No. You know, you'd be the first person I'd call."

"I need to tell you something. Myers is missing too. He told me he was going camping with Tim, but he lied. I saw Tim last night in Charlotte. I think Myers is with Casey. And I think we've found a lead."

"Oh my God, Susannah!"

"I've been talking to Chase about all this. I cracked Myers's Facebook password and looked at his contacts and messages. You know, my niece Sloan lives in New York and she sent Myers a message on Tuesday that said, 'Package arrived!' and I think she meant Casey."

"Wait—you've lost me." She sounds unconvinced, stalling my momentum.

"Well, Chase and I have been talking about the case, and he had the idea that maybe Casey went to New York, wanting to audition for some shows. We looked at the auditions that are taking place in New York this week and we found one or two that looked like winners."

"Shows? Wait—what? When did you and Chase talk? He's supposed to be keeping me in the loop." She sounds anxious.

I take a deep breath. "I was with him last night when I saw Tim. That was when I realized Myers had gone away...well, somewhere else.

Anyway, after I'd confronted Tim, asking where Myers was, Chase and I came back here and went through Casey's Facebook contacts, and he got the idea that she might have gone up there."

"Wow."

"And then this morning, when I looked at Myers's messages, I found my niece going by a weird alias, *Velveeta Cheeser*."

"You mean the full-figure model, right?"

"Yes. Chase thought that since Casey had met her, and had been in *Hairspray*, that Sloan might be an inspiration, being a full-figured girl as well. We found a message on Casey's page from Sloan back in April, offering her a place to crash if she wanted to come to New York. I called Sloan, but she didn't answer her phone."

"Okay. I'm sitting down. This is all starting to make sense."

"Chase has a P.I. friend in New York running down some leads. Chase has been up most of the night working on it. He's going to have his friend try to run down Sloan. Maybe he'll find Casey."

"Well, wow! I don't know what to say. Why didn't you call me?"

"It was late and there was nothing you could do, except stay up all night worrying. Chase will call you the minute he hears from his friend."

There is silence as Maggie processes what I've told her.

"You must be worried sick about Myers."

"Well, I know he's not in a New York hospital, and he's not showing up on any police reports—neither is Casey. If our hunch is right, we should know something soon. I think he's helping Casey, and I believe if they were really in trouble, they'd call. Like I said, Chase is following up."

"Oh! This is so awful! The not knowing is the worst feeling. And if Casey has gotten Myers in trouble, I'm going to kill her!"

"Let's not jump to conclusions."

"Are you kidding? That's all we *are* doing. Have you called your sister to see if she knows anything?"

"Yes, and she's as clueless as ever. She and Sloan don't communicate at all anymore, so it seems."

"That's sad."

"I know."

"Wait a minute—did you just say you were with Chase last night?"

"Yes." *Oh boy, here it comes.* "It—he asked me out for a drink to talk about his wife, and how I haven't moved on with Stan. He hasn't moved on from Patti either, so it was all kind of sad, and then we saw Tim and all hell broke loose."

"Hmm."

"Listen, before you start getting the wrong idea, what are you doing for lunch?"

"Well, nothing I guess. Callum came back into town last night, and he and Ed have taken his car in to get new tires and a check-up before he has to go back to school. I'm free right now. Please save me. I was getting ready to clean my bathrooms!"

"In that case, come on over! We can at least go out of our minds together! One of my patients brought me fresh tomatoes. We can fix a tomato sandwich and eat out on the front porch. It's not so hot today."

"Perfect. Can you give me a couple of hours? I really do need to clean these bathrooms."

"Okay, just come over whenever you're ready. I'm sticking close to home."

Hoping for better luck this time, I place another call to Sloan's phone number, but again, I get her voicemail. I try Myers again too, to no avail. I don't even bother to leave a message. He'll see that I've called.

I, too, should busy myself with household chores to keep my mind occupied, I think, following Maggie's example. Doing a load of laundry is first on my list, and I scan my bedroom for running wear and other items I can wash. A nagging urge tugs at me as I pass Stan's closet door. I stop and open the door, thinking today could be the day that I pack up his clothes and donate them to a charity. I hang his robe back on the hook inside the closet and close the door. No. I can't handle it today. I'd rather tackle Myers's room—or not! I wade through the clothes on the floor of his room, sorting the clean from the dirty ones, wishing he were here so I could yell at him about his awful room. I start a load of laundry and change the sheets on his bed. Maybe in all this mess, I will uncover a clue. *Where are you, Myers?*

Remembering I haven't gotten yesterday's mail, I walk out to check the mailbox. Bills and junk mail dominate the pile, so I deposit it on the porch table and proceed to pinch the brown leaves and spent blossoms off of my geraniums. I go back inside to slice tomatoes for lunch. Peeking at the house next door to see whether anyone is there, I make tea and rinse purple grapes at the sink. Then I call Mark Miller to check on his mother, and I get a good report. He tells me she is starting to come around and the nurses have had her up and walking. She has eaten some pudding and her speech is more coherent. Fang is doing well. It's all good news and my mood is lifted.

I try both of the other calls again, wondering how many times Maggie has called Casey and gotten nothing.

Eventually, Maggie strolls up my walkway and we hug each other like long lost friends. She's brought flowers from her garden, the last of the pale peach lilies that I always gush about.

"Oh, thank you! These are beautiful!"

"I thought we could both use some cheering up."

"Definitely! Come on in. I've sliced these delicious-looking tomatoes, and we can put together our sandwiches. Would you like some iced tea?"

"Sure," she says, pouring our tea while I find the right vase and arrange my flowers. In moments, we are at the table on the front porch, eating our sandwiches and enjoying the lilies while my young neighbors make happy noises in their backyard on the other side of my house.

I tell Maggie about Fang coming over and alerting me to Mrs. Miller, and then come clean about Chase's ride-along.

"I think Detective Chase has a thing for you," she says, squeezing lemon into her tea.

"No, he doesn't. I explained what that was all about. He just needs a fellow widow to commiserate with is all it is."

"Yeah. I saw him checking out your legs that night you had on the red shoes."

"Well, I don't mean this in any kind of haughty, conceited way, but I was pretty awkward looking in a distracting sort of way, and he is alive, and he is a man. I don't think for one minute that he's available, so please don't go there, okay?"

"He's also adorable. Shoot girl, he's hangin' my moon and I'm *married!* And you are a beautiful woman. But I won't go there." She gives me a sly smile and changes the subject. "These tomatoes are dee-*licious!* These are the first homegrown tomatoes I've had this summer. Ed's tomatoes won't be ready for at least another week."

A car pulls up to my curb, attracting our attention. It's Jen. And Kent.

"Oh, God," I mutter, wondering what's up.

They open their doors and climb out quickly, shutting the doors abruptly, and walk up the sidewalk and up my steps. Kent walks with a swagger that is supposed to tell us he's something special. He runs a hand over his fashionably neat beard. He has always reminded me of Sir Walter Raleigh without the fancy collar; I don't know why.

"Hi. You guys remember Maggie."

"Hey, Maggie!" Jen greets her, while Kent nods and says hello to both of us politely. Maggie and Kent don't know each other well. Fortunately for her, Maggie came into my life after I'd married Stan. Jen hugs me. She looks great as usual, and she transfers a lethal amount of Obsession onto me from our contact. It's not my favorite fragrance, but I'm wearing it now.

"Did you get in touch with Sloan?" Jen begins abruptly.

"No. She didn't answer her phone. I called several times."

"So did I, and I couldn't reach her either."

"Would she be working on a Saturday?" asks Maggie.

Jen shrugs. "Who knows? I think her schedule is pretty erratic."

Kent looks at me with an urgency he didn't display last night.

"No word from Myers?" he asks, and I wonder when it hit him that Myers's disappearance is a serious thing.

"No. And I've called him frequently as well."

"So have I," he says, verifying my lack of success. "What do you all think is going on?" he asks.

I gesture for them to sit down in the other chairs around the table. "Would y'all like some tea?"

"No, thank you," they answer in unison.

I explain the events as best as I can recall, and Maggie chimes in helpfully when I have left something out. When they are up to speed, Kent shakes his head.

"You're really stretching this theory out, don't you think?"

"What else could they be up to? They're all tied into this in some way and none of them is answering a phone. Something is going on, and I think Myers followed Casey to New York to help her out."

"Have you seen the size of Sloan's apartment?" Jen asks, unwilling to believe my conjectures as well. "I mean, there's hardly enough room for her and her roommate, much less two more people," she says, gesturing with her hand for emphasis.

"I didn't imply that anyone is comfortable. I just think that's where they are."

We are quiet for a moment. I think about asking Kent where he was last night when another car comes around the corner and pulls up behind Jen's car. It's Chase. He pops out of his car and dashes up the stairs.

"Hey!" he says, and I can tell that he has not shaved or possibly even slept since I saw him last night. He's wearing the same shirt and slacks from last night as well.

"Hi!" I am so glad to see him, and he looks like he has news. He looks questioningly at the newcomers. "Detective Chase, this is my sister Jen, Sloan's mother, and this is Kent Morgan, Myers's father."

They greet one another and shake hands. Chase regards them politely, but looks momentarily confused with all the relationships going on here. It is obvious by Kent's hand massaging the back of Jen's neck that they are *together*. I will have to explain it to him another time.

He presses on with his news. We stand in a huddle on my front porch as if we are a football team getting ready to run a Hail Mary.

"I looked back through all the train station manifests, thinking I was missing something. And then, when we realized that Sloan was using an alias, and y'all had said Casey liked to play with stage names, I started looking for other names that might ring a bell."

"Like *Chardonnay French*," Maggie says.

"Exactly. And Susannah, she said she liked your name. So I found a name on the manifest that really stood out: *Savannah Myers*. I don't know why it didn't jump out at me before. There was a Savannah Myers who took the train from Charlotte to New York on Monday."

We all gasp.

"Wait—she'd need a picture ID to board a train," Kent points out, hands on hips like he's ready to take Chase on.

"Could have used a fake ID. Lots of teenagers have them." Chase shrugs, making Maggie close her eyes and sigh. One more bad move.

"There's more. I had my buddy, the private investigator in New York, follow up on a couple of things. First, nobody was home at Sloan's address. Then, he went to the theater where they are holding auditions for *Plus Size*—"

"That's a play in New York," I add for the latecomers.

"He just left the theater. He showed her picture to the director, and the guy said Casey was there on Wednesday. He said she looked different though, pretty—blonder hair and more made-up looking than in the picture I sent, but the director was sure it was her. Said she was great, too, and she had a callback."

"She got a *callback*? When was it?" asks Maggie, hanging on every word.

"It was this morning, but she didn't show."

The four of us are speechless. *Where are they?* Kent turns to pace the porch, stroking his beard, while Maggie sinks into her chair. Jen does the same thing while I stand, facing Chase, my mind racing. Our eyes lock, those moss green ones of his searing into mine.

"They're in trouble," I say. *The understatement of the day.*

"I think so. My buddy is checking the hospitals in the city again—this time for any one of the three of them."

My stomach drops like a rock and adrenaline suddenly pumps its way through my veins, like a dam that's just burst. I have to take charge, and I know exactly what I need to do. I look away from Chase, glancing at the others.

"Okay, I'm going inside to get on my computer and call the airlines. Maggie, I'm going to buy us two plane tickets. Girl, you and I are going to New York. *Today.*"

"Oh, hell yeah!" Maggie says, scrambling to her feet, eyes wide. Chase's eyebrows ratchet up a notch and I return his look. There's nothing so rewarding as seeing the glint in his eye that tells me he likes my idea.

"Damn right," he says, setting his strong face into utter resolve and putting his hands on his hips while Kent opens and closes his mouth completely ineffectively, trying to catch up. I'm reminded of a toad catching flies! Chase goes on, obviously sharing my rush.

"Get three tickets. I'm going with you. That is, if you want my company," Chase adds, looking as if he's thoroughly prepared to drop everything, squeal out of my neighborhood on two wheels, and drive us to the airport with nary a shaving kit nor a change of clothes. *Now.* He's sending me an unmistakable vibe that he's in this with me. This is the way he rolls. I'm catapulted to that pain and pleasure juncture again. The thought of the two of us sitting in the close proximity only airplane seats can afford sends a decisive quiver throughout my insides, making me suck in air, and forcing me to look away from him. I am supposed to be consumed by worry over my son, but this hot and commanding detective in front of me is making it mighty hard to concentrate! *Help me, Jesus!*

"I've got to call Ed," says Maggie, lifting her phone out of her pocket at the same moment my phone rings.

"It's Myers!"

Before I can answer, Maggie's phone rings next. "Oh! Thank God, it's Casey," she whispers.

Chapter 15

SOME EXPLAINING TO DO

"Mom. Don't get upset. I'm with Casey. She's fine, but...."

"Myers, where are you?" I ask, trying to listen to Maggie's conversation with Casey as well. She puts her finger in her ear and walks away from me so she can hear Casey.

"We're at the hospital with Sloan...in New York. We've got to call Aunt Jen," he says and I can hear him trying to control the panic in his voice. Maggie turns her eyes back to me and has just heard the same news. I look at Jen, whose hand goes to her mouth. She can hear Myers's voice from my phone, even as hoarse as it is. Kent places his hand under her elbow. I beckon to Maggie to come over.

"They're in New York—at a hospital with Sloan," I say to the others. "Myers, I'm going to put you on speaker so we can all hear you better. Detective Chase is here, and so are Maggie, and your dad, and Jen. Just tell us what's going on."

Maggie is at my side, instructing Casey to do the same thing, and telling her who is listening. We're huddling again, and Chase looks at me, then Maggie, and then Jen, perhaps wondering which one of us will fall over first!

"Okay…I came up here Thursday because Casey was staying here with Sloan. She said Sloan was sick and she didn't know what to do. Sloan didn't want to go to the doctor because she doesn't have health insurance, but Casey said she was getting worse and worse. By the time I got up here, she was pale and clammy and feeling really awful. She kept drinking sodas and eating bagels, trying to settle her stomach, but she didn't have any energy. This morning she wasn't any better, and when she tried to stand up, she passed out, so we called 911. The EMS guys asked us if Sloan's a diabetic and I told them I didn't know."

Jen's eyes are wide and she shakes her head.

"No. Jen's shaking her head."

"We're at the hospital right now. The doctor says her blood sugar's like—really super-high. She said Sloan's in a diabetic coma," Myers says, gulping with fear.

"Oh, Myers!" I don't know where to begin. It's so strange, knowing we were right on their heels, but to find out that it's all really true is hard to take in. "Wh—why haven't you called? Where have you and Casey been staying?" is all I can think to ask him.

"We've been at Sloan's place. Her roommate's never there, so we've been sleeping on a blow-up mattress."

"But you're both okay?"

"Yeah, we're just so worried about Sloan."

"Type 2 diabetes," I murmur, for Jen's benefit.

"Yeah! That's what the doctor called it. She said it was probably adult onset diabetes."

"It's the same thing."

"Sloan wasn't able to talk or tell her anything, but that's what she thinks it is. She said Sloan probably didn't even know she had it, but that it runs in families."

Jen's eyes are wide, and she sits down at the table. Chase hands her my iced tea, and she drinks it.

"Yes. It does, but we don't know that much about Jen's family history. And her father, well...."

Jen shakes her head. "He never mentioned it," she says.

"I feel so bad!" Casey's emotional voice comes over the phone. "When I got here, Sloan and I had a Twinkie fest and I think that's when she started feeling bad."

"Well, that probably didn't help matters, but I'm sure it probably wasn't just the Twinkies that caused Sloan's problems," I say. "Type 2 diabetes takes years of bad eating habits and lack of exercise to cultivate. Plus, it has a lot to do with a person's body type and genetic disposition as well. What is the doctor saying? Is Sloan beginning to come out of it? How long have you all been at the hospital?"

"We've been here—what, Myers, about an hour?"

"Yeah," he says. "She's still kinda out of it. I was getting ready to call you, Aunt Jen. You were next on the list."

We all roll our eyes. Why did they wait? *Why did they do anything they've done?* This could have been a much worse disaster, and totally avoidable. Kent looks like he is going to start in on Myers.

"You should have called as soon as you got there, Myers," he says in his most caustic tone, the one I know so well.

"That's not helping," I say as calmly as I can.

"He's been *lying* to you, Susannah," Kent continues, as if lying is something I've allowed and perhaps condoned on a regular basis. I have half a mind to remind him who's the biggest liar in the family, but I refrain.

Chase's phone rings and he steps away to answer it. It must be his private eye friend with the news we already know. Chase speaks to him briefly, bringing him up to speed from our end, thanking him, and promising to get back to him later. Maggie and Casey resume their private conversation, while Myers speaks to Jen, giving her the doctor's name and Sloan's room number at the hospital. She gets a pen from her purse, writes down all the details, and then puts Myers back on the phone with me.

Four hours later, Maggie, Jen, and I are sitting on an airplane, heading for JFK. I feel shell-shocked, sitting in my seat beside Jen. The man beside me was kind enough to switch seats with her so we could sit together. We were lucky to get on the same flight. I can hear Maggie talking to the woman beside her, two rows back on the other side of the aisle. To me, she sounds nervous, but the new woman won't know. Our plan came together effortlessly. We will fly up, spend the night in a hotel, and then Maggie, Casey, and I will drive back with Myers tomorrow. Jen will stay with Sloan until she can get her settled, and then fly back whenever she is ready. *I can't believe my son has driven to New York City.* As angry and irritated as I am with him for lying to me, and running off without my knowledge, I have to admit I'm proud of him in an offhand way for commandeering this mission.

We're all mad at them, but they are our children, so what can we do but go up there and bail them out? Maggie got an earful from Casey about the auditions. Her overall experience was more overwhelming than she'd anticipated, and she has learned that even though she was successful at getting a callback, New York City scares her to death and she is not ready for the kind of life she's seen. We were glad that she had the sense to stick by Sloan and call Myers for reinforcement, abandoning the auditions for Sloan's care, which was more important. Chase pointed out that if Casey had not gone to New York, Sloan could have gotten herself into a dangerous situation with no one around to help her out. That silenced my ex-husband, who spent the rest of the visit flexing his jaw muscle and cracking his knuckles.

I sit back in my seat, closing my eyes, so grateful to Chase for helping us figure it all out. After we had all thanked him, however inadequately, he'd graciously backed out of the trip, understanding our mission was now just a family's errand to go and retrieve our children. He'd slipped out discretely when our families began working out the details of our rescue mission. It was exhilarating in that moment when I thought we'd be together for all the excitement of tracking down Myers and Casey, like falling down a rabbit hole with him, but then again, I know I was just being especially privy to one of his professional highs. I allowed myself one more time to get caught up in a thrilling fantasy I have no business entertaining. So I let my doctor's good sense take over and watched him walk down my sidewalk, slip quietly into his car, and disappear—quite slowly—around the corner.

I don't suppose I'll see Chase again, unless he's out jogging when I am, and I'm more disappointed about it than I want to admit. I will miss the exciting side of him, and the roller coaster of emotions he brings out in me. I'm imagining seeing him out in the village, pumping gas at the station around the corner or bumping into him in the grocery store. How will we be with each other, now that the thrill of the hunt is over? Will he just wave and move on his way like it used to be before this case? What was lost between us? Was there anything there to lose, or am I just imagining things? I know that he was intriguing to me for reasons other than the professional workings of Myers and Casey's case. Why is it when that little female voice inside me cried out for the third or fourth time, I heard her clearly but squashed her yet again? I may never know the answer to that question. Could I have done anything to change it? That kind of action would have required more courage than I apparently have, no matter how well I liked the drama. If nothing else, Chase and I were simply victims of bad timing. Even mere companionship would have been nice; I certainly liked him well enough. But the way he slipped away off my porch earlier, I got the disappointing feeling he is through with me. He was just working a case after all.

Sighing dismissively, I turn my attention to my sister, someone who may really need me. Jen must be going out of her mind, I think, as I watch her, reading about Sloan's disease on her phone screen. What did we do without these pesky little devices in the past?

She sees me looking and puts the phone down. "How did you know about Kent?"

"What?" Her seemingly unrelated question catches me completely off-guard.

"Back when you found out he was having an affair…how did you find out?"

I laugh. It's another irony about our fascination with technology. Still, she must be on to him. I've noticed there has been no engagement announcement. I would never say, *I told you so*, and if she's figured out his game, I'm happy for her, even though it probably hurts. She waits for my story. I think back to 2002.

"Well…it was back when everyone started texting. Kent had just gotten a new Blackberry. I had a flip phone, but I thought texting was hard, just using the number pad, so he'd shown me how to do it on his phone and it was a lot easier. He said his paralegal, Penny, was teaching him. Anyway, I started noticing that he was starting to keep his phone in his jacket pocket. He worked late a lot, and one night he came home and was taking a shower. I walked by the closet door and heard his phone buzzing, so I found it in his pocket and checked to see who was calling him. It was a text from Dirty Penny. It said, 'Sure enjoyed working late with you on Naked vs. Naked! I'm still out of breath!' And I could smell her on his clothes."

Jen looks grave. "There were more messages?"

"Oh, yeah. Most of them were much more provocative than that. I took pictures of all of them. One morning, he couldn't find his phone because I'd taken it. I'd cleared out a day and made an appointment with my lawyer ahead of time. While he was at work, I showed her what he was up to. I told her all about the night he'd thrown that beer bottle at my head…." Jen knows this story. My lawyer was one of the top divorce attorneys in Charlotte, and Kent was well aware that she was. "She said I had a slam-dunk case. When I told him that I'd been to see Castrating Kim Callahan, and what I'd shown her, he went white. It was an easy settlement after that. He didn't fight me on anything. I told him he could have half of the sale of our house, and it would be up to the judge how much contact he could have with Myers after the beer bottle thing. Stan encouraged me to press charges, and I was glad I did. I didn't want anything else from Kent. I just wanted out, and he had no choice but to cooperate."

I gaze at Jen as she takes in my story. I'd told her most of this before, but I suppose she needed to hear it again. She'd seemed so disinterested at the time. Finally, she looks at me.

"I think it's over with him, Susannah. I'm sure he's doing the same things again, with me. I think he was going to tell me about it this morning when he came over, but then, all this happened with Sloan…. And he didn't even offer to help me out with it all. That, in and of itself, is the biggest red flag for me."

"I'm sorry, Jen."

"Don't be. I'm definitely the one who should be sorry. For so much. If I'd been in contact with Sloan more, maybe none of this would have happened. And as for Kent, I can't believe what I've been doing. Looking back on it all, it was crazy getting involved with him. I don't know why I deluded myself all this time. And I know it was painful for you."

"Awkward, but not painful. But I'm glad for your sake that it's over."

"Absolutely. I'm so over him. You know, I've watched you a lot over the last three years since Stan died. He was really wonderful. You've handled yourself with such grace and strength. You're a good mother; just look at Myers. You have the kind of strength I don't believe I have."

"You might surprise yourself, but thank you," I say, reaching over to squeeze her hand, feeling surprise and relief flood through me. I feel surprise that she's come to these realizations on her own. I feel relief for Jen, for me, and for Myers, not to mention our poor parents! Kent can stay on the back burner where he belongs, and where he has conveniently placed himself again. Hopefully, Jen can focus on her family, and she and Sloan can reconnect and repair their broken bond. She's already been on the phone, trying to do the same with Trip. It's nice to have my sister back. "Sloan will be okay. We're all going to be okay."

"I think so. Thank you."

After a grueling evening at the hospital where we found all three children (Myers and Casey having nowhere else to go), we've finally managed to collapse in our two-bedroom hotel suite, where we have ordered room service. I am shaking from hunger as I bite into my club sandwich. We are all feeling hungry and exhausted, I think, as I watch Myers wolf down a cheeseburger. After our air travel, shuttle service to the hotel, and then a cab ride to the hospital, Maggie and I realized we had not eaten since the tomato sandwiches earlier in the day. Also, being in Sloan's room, and focusing our attention on the attributes of eating the right foods at the appropriate times to maintain healthy blood sugar levels, our hunger has intensified noticeably. One thing that has been abated is our anxiety about our kids. Sloan is recovering, sleeping off her ordeal in the hospital, so the rest of us are going to stay here tonight. I feel my body relaxing with each bite. It was such a relief to lay eyes on all three of them, and getting my arms around Myers made me realize how upset I was. But I am still mad at him. We have yet to get the whole story.

Casey is quieter than usual. She looks so different—older at least. Her hair, a lighter shade of blond, has been styled noticeably, although in the wake of her vigil over Sloan, it has fallen into lank waves around her face.

She wears makeup from this morning, when she thought she'd be going to her casting callback, before Sloan took a turn for the worse, which changed everything. She eats her sandwich silently, probably wanting to avoid the inevitable conversation that Maggie is about to start.

Maggie wipes the crumbs off her fingers and wads her napkin, tossing it onto her plate. "This is not the way I like to see the Big Apple," she says, and I laugh at her understatement. Jen is too tired and sensitive to see the humor and feels a little guilty, so she watches me for my reactions to my friend. Maggie continues, "So, Case, tell us what in the world you were thinking and how you cooked up this plan of yours." She sits back on the couch, crossing her arms and legs—not a good sign if you are eighteen and in serious trouble.

Casey casts her eyes at Myers, who regards her with lips pressed together. He is not happy with her either, but still, he's an accomplice, so I have zero sympathy for him.

"Okay...Mom, first let me just say that getting out of this was way harder than getting into it was...."

It's an honest beginning, and it reminds me of Fang. *Coming down should be just as easy as going up,* but maybe not, even for people. Crap! Fang. I'd forgotten that I volunteered to take care of him when Mark and Brenda leave tomorrow, so I'll need to call them on our trip back in the car. Thirteen-and-a-half long hours!

"Who took you to the train station and where did you get the fake ID?" Maggie asks.

"Spencer took me...before he and his family went on vacation."

"And the ID?"

Casey shrugs, avoiding the question, probably hoping not to incriminate anyone. Spencer may have some explaining to do as well when he returns to this country.

"I thought I could come up here and crash with Sloan and check out the audition process."

"Honey! What did you think would happen if you got a part? What were you going to do—skip college?" Maggie cries, hands lifted in disbelief.

"Mom! I didn't think I'd get a part! I never thought in a billion years I'd even get a callback! I *was* planning to come back home next week. But I had to try it out, Mom. I needed to see if anyone else thought I was good enough. You and Dad weren't on board with my acting, but I knew I had to be good at it if other people liked me as much as they did. And I was going to call you yesterday and tell you all about it, but then Sloan got worse."

Maggie's mouth is hanging open. So is mine.

"Honey...!" Maggie is flabbergasted. The rant begins. "I'm glad you got to find out.... But! Bad choices! This all boils down to making poor choices again, Casey... You were so sneaky about it, going to such lengths to cover your tracks. And having that fake ID with an alias? Do you know how serious that is? Oh, I'm sorry, it was a *stage name!* You could be in big trouble for that. It's probably a misdemeanor. It could be fraud! I don't even know."

"We know a good lawyer," Myers says, shrugging, drawing disdainful looks from all three of us mothers.

"Casey, y-you had to have known what you were doing was more than wrong! Can you even imagine how worried we've all been? We've had the *police* looking for you!" Maggie says, unable to think of what else to say. Jen looks unfazed. This is nothing compared to what her kids have done! Still, Sloan's illness sits largely in the room with us.

"I know, Mom. I'm so sorry. I knew you and Dad would never have let me go. I've been planning it for a long time. I know you're both really upset with me. I'm so sorry. Believe me, I've really learned my lesson this time."

"Have you?"

Casey nods. I'm wondering what kind of punishment would be effective on these two, in light of the fact that they're leaving for college in a month. Do you *ground* college students? Maybe Chase can arrest them!

Now it is my turn to glare at Myers and he braces himself for what is coming.

"How long have you known about all this?" My tone sounds harsher than I'd intended, but we're all so tired, we can hardly function.

"Saturday. When we got back from camp. I was unpacking and I found that trac phone in my suitcase." He turns to Casey. "That was a little too *Mission Impossible* for me when I got the first call from you," he says curtly. "You know, getting the word about what my mission was. I wasn't too comfortable covering for you. Especially when all hell broke loose and I had to come up here and bail you out. Look, I know you were scared being up here by yourself and getting caught up in Sloan's nightmare…and I'm glad you called me for moral support, but do you know how freakin' hard it is to drive around up here?" He glares at her. I can only imagine—my son driving all the way up here on his own and navigating New York City traffic!

"Why didn't you just tell me what was going on?" My hands are in my hair, I am so frustrated with them. "Why did you lie to me?"

Myers flounders for a moment, searching for what to say.

"Okay, it was stupid, all of it. And I'm sorry I lied. I knew Casey would have to come home if you knew, and if Maggie and Ed knew where she was. I wanted her to go after her dream, Mom. You and Stan always encouraged me to go after mine. After Casey got busted, it looked like her dreams were over, so I wanted to help her. I was trying to be her friend. She said so many times how much she hates living in Magnolia and she just wanted to break out and do her own thing—her own way. I didn't like lying about it, but I wanted her to have a chance to try. You did it for me, letting me go to Belmont…Nashville…it's everything I want.

We should all go for it—find our happiness, including you, Mom. You need to break out too."

My eyes are wide. How can he throw this back at me? What is he talking about? *My love-life?* We are all staring at him. And then Casey smirks. She tries to hide her face, but a smile forms behind her hands, and suddenly, she is overcome with her characteristic giggles. Now we are staring at her. She cannot control herself and the result makes her laugh harder.

"I'm sorry! You just told your mom to *break out.* That's so funny! She's a dermatologist!"

She is into full-fledge machine gun laughter now, and Jen is the first to react. She snorts, and Maggie laughs next. Myers looks at Casey with good-natured disgust at her bad joke, and he gives her arm a shove, making her sink back into her chair.

Jen stands and collects our plates. "Well, Sloan has some explaining to do as well. She should never have let you come up here under the radar like you did," she says to Casey. There is no use questioning Sloan's motives. Sloan did the same thing after college, coming up here to be the rebellious one, and as her luck would have it, she was able to stay and pursue her own dreams.

"She wanted to help me too," Casey says, sobering up quickly, wiping her eyes. "She said as long as I could take care of myself, she'd let me stay for a couple of weeks and sleep on her inflatable bed."

"But you didn't think you'd have to take care of *her*," Myers says in Casey's defense.

"Well, no. I could tell as soon as I got up here that she wasn't well. Her eating habits are disgusting. I don't think she's ever met a vegetable." Casey sends an apologetic look to Jen. "She worked a couple of days, and then laid around, feeling bad. I thought she just had a virus or something, but it got worse, and she wouldn't go to the doctor, so I called Myers to come and help. She wasn't listening to me. I thought maybe he could convince her to go…and I was freaking out here! Her roommate had left to go to Montauk for the holiday weekend, and I don't think she realized how sick Sloan was getting. I was so scared!"

"I wish you'd called me," says Jen.

"She asked me not to," Casey says, eyes cutting to the floor. Jen shrugs. Sloan and Jen have always butted heads. Still, it's hard being rejected as a mother. I had a small taste of that myself and did not like it.

"Well, we'll have thirteen or fourteen hours to discuss all this further in the car tomorrow on the way home. I suggest we get some sleep so we can get an early start, since we have so much to do in the morning," Maggie says, looking at Myers and Casey. Our plan is to stop by the apartment on the way out, get their things, and drop Jen off so she can settle in before going to the hospital. She has never been to New York by herself and knows no one here. I think she feels a bit daunted by what lies ahead. This will be her chance to break out too, I suppose. Not having Kent for moral support will be hard for Jen, but that is her choice now. No one said breaking out would be easy. And some of us have less courage than others.

Chapter 16

PACKING

Myers seems completely uninterested in choosing the bedding for his dorm, or helping me make a list of the clothes he'll need at college, considering he'll be there until Thanksgiving, when he can come home and switch out his summer clothes for winter coats. After assembling as many pairs of pants and shirts as I can imagine he'll need, aside from his casual summer clothes, he picks up his violin and shoos me out of his room with his bow.

"Okay, I can take a hint," I say as he starts up a fiddle tune that reminds me of a train's whistle as it's coming down the tracks. The "Orange Blossom Special" is about to leave his bedroom.

"We've got three weeks, Mom," he laughs.

"Yes, we do, and I know exactly what's going to happen. You'll wait three weeks and then panic because you haven't thought of everything you need to do. Then I'll have the last laugh and pull out one of my famous lists!"

He chuckles, playing louder.

I wander back to my bedroom, wondering what I'll wear to Maggie's tonight. We've been invited to a late dinner. It's not a celebration, she reminded me, since Myers and Casey are enduring some kind of punishment for their transgressions, as they should. This Tuesday night supper is not being billed as some kind of prodigal son's return to the fold for a *kill-the-fatted-calf* kind of thing. No, no, it's just friends having dinner together. Besides, why should the adults suffer?

The July heat has returned with a vengeance, so I think I'll wear shorts and sandals. It's just the Frenchs, after all. I stop at my closet and turn, looking at the opposite door. *It's time*, I think, my own voice giving the suggestion this time. Opening Stan's closet, I lean in to smell one more time, running my fingers along the sleeve of his leather jacket. I'll keep this for Myers, and of course, the bathrobe will stay, but all the rest is going. Reaching up, I clasp as many hangers as I can, lifting the clothes carefully out and taking them to my bed. I repeat the process until all the clothes are laid across the bed. I am on a roll now, I think, as I listen to Myers playing a lively Celtic tune. I'm glad he's chosen something upbeat; the last thing I need is a depressing, melancholy ballad.

In minutes, I've made stacks of folded shirts, slacks, ties, belts, and shoes. Sweaters go in another pile to be counted and itemized on notebook paper for my tax deduction record. I slip out into the kitchen for a moment, finding the plastic garbage bags I need to pack everything away. It takes less than ten minutes to bag the garments and load them neatly in the back of my car. Back in the kitchen, I finish my list and tuck it into my tax folder, sighing deeply. There. That wasn't so bad. All I have to do is stop by the charity store and drop them off and I will be done with the last vestiges of my husband.

Except the ring. My head hangs as I twist the three-part band on my finger. *It's okay*, I tell myself, knowing that a little guilt would follow this moment. I'll tell Maggie about it tonight; she'll absolve me of the guilt, and then I can move on. Oh, I need my friend! After another deep breath, I can make myself go on to the next task. Startling me, Fang appears, winding himself softly between my ankles to announce it is time to eat. I forgot that he was here. I'm not used to having him around. I pick him up and snuggle him under my neck before placing him back on the floor and filling his bowls with fresh food and water.

Mark called earlier to tell me that Mrs. Miller was going to be moved to the rehab floor of the hospital and would be there for about a month. He thanked me in advance for taking care of her cat, but I am glad to have Fang around. Having him here will be a good trial run for me to see how I do with a pet. If I want to travel, I can certainly hire a pet sitter, or look into the local kennel. There is no reason I should be by myself when Myers leaves for Nashville.

Thinking I have time for a quick shower before I change out of my work clothes, I start back to my bedroom when I hear a knock at my door. If Tim has come by to hang out with Myers, I will have to send him on his way. He wouldn't have the nerve—not now, anyway—so who could this be? I open the door to find Chase standing on my doorstep, as usual, a respectful distance away. My insides do a little flip and a flutter, both of which I try to ignore.

"Chase. Hi!"

"Hi, Susannah. I was on my way home from work and thought I'd drop this off," he says, producing a key from his pocket.

"Oh! Of course! Mrs. Miller's spare key."

"Yeah, Mark had given it to me when he wasn't sure you'd be back from New York in time to take over with Fang, so…."

"Oh, right."

"Yeah, I stopped by on Sunday to check on everything over there and he gave it to me."

"Oh, I guess he didn't realize that I have one of my own. I—should have called you…"

"No, not at all. I knew you had an extra key. You had a lot on your plate," he says, handing me the key.

I swallow. "Well, it all worked out all right. Everyone's okay now, all safe and sound. Thanks for everything you did."

"You're welcome. How's Sloan doing?"

"She's much better. Jen is flying in tonight, and my parents are picking her up at the airport. I think she and Sloan had a really good visit and they were able to make some amends for their past differences."

"Good. And the kids?"

"Oh, they're both for sale!" I blurt, making him laugh. "Well, Casey is still alive. Ed didn't kill her after all. She and Myers are both grounded," I say with a chuckle. "Actually, grounding them seems like nothing after what they've pulled. We were, uh…hoping you could arrest them…."

He chuckles, watching me with a new deep, tender gaze that's making it hard to breathe.

"Have you heard about Mrs. Miller today?" I ask, barely able to speak. I try to make myself sound normal. He's still watching me. "I just got home a little bit ago, but I talked to Mark earlier." Maybe if I stick to a normal topic, he won't notice I'm nervous.

"I did, too. He said they moved her to the rehab floor today, and I guess she'll be there for a few weeks. Day-to-day, you know? Like you said."

"Yeah. That's good. Mark said she was making some steady gains." Suddenly aware that it's awkward, both of us standing on my porch this way, I ask, "Would you like to come in?"

"Oh, no. I know you've got things to do. I just wanted to drop off the key, and…to give you something else."

"What?"

He fishes in his pocket and pulls out a small object. It is then that I notice he's not wearing his ring. He hands me a small, creamy porcelain box with a hinged lid. There are flowers painted on the lid, with a little gold trim around the edge. It's quite lovely and thoughtful, especially when he says the next part.

"Olivia has one of these. I was in Charlotte, working on a case, and I had to wait around in a gift shop to talk to the clerk. This was staring at me from the counter, so I got one for myself and one for you. I thought that someday you might have use for it. It's a ring box." He rubs his thumb across the smooth surface of the lid.

My eyes lift toward his, and his face is gentler than I've ever seen it.

"Oh…. You took off your ring."

"Yes, I did. I figured it was about time." He hands me the box.

"But you were going to wait until you went to California. At least, that's what I thought. Until you could sit on that bench under the tree, to see if…."

"Susannah…" he says softly, and the moss green eyes search back and forth over mine. He takes a deep breath. "I don't need to sit on a bench to know what I want."

I blink at him, but he stares me down. It's unnerving but delightful at the same time. I feel my insides quivering again. He takes a step closer.

Then he gives the slightest of shrugs. "They'd want us to be happy…. *I* want to be happy. Don't you?"

"Yes," I whisper. It's all I can manage. He smiles. Suddenly, I recall having to be somewhere, but I push it quickly from my mind, wanting nothing except for this conversation to continue. I feel an addiction building in me like a wave swelling in the ocean, slow and strong with only one outcome.

He raises a hand to my face and traces his thumb across my cheek.

"I've been wanting to do this for a while, and I think it's time…" he says and leans in to kiss me. It's soft and sweet. I find myself kissing him back. Oddly, it feels so familiar, and I realize I've imagined it more than once. It's even better than I thought it would be. He begins to draw away, but then he kisses me again; this time it's purposeful and lingering. I can feel the longing in it, from both of us. There is almost a *whoosh* when we pull apart and our foreheads touch before our eyes meet again, and I feel as though we've jumped over an abyss. *The Grand Canyon.*

It takes a moment for us to adjust. I like where we are now—on the roof together, with no idea how to get back down. But I'm okay with it.

"We had a terrible first date, didn't we?" he asks.

"Yes. Well…not all of it was bad. But you thought so too?"

"I guess our timing was just…off. Do you think we could give it another shot?"

I nod. "We should."

"Okay," he says, sounding pleased, letting his hand fall away from my face. I think he is getting ready to turn and go, but then he lifts a finger and says, "There's just one thing I want, the next time we go out."

My interest is definitely piqued. His eyes drop to my feet and then slowly back up.

He hesitates for just a moment, and then he asks shyly, "Would you wear those red shoes for me?" He looks as if he is holding his breath.

I remember the way he looked at me that day in Maggie's doorway and her words, *You could have some hot dates with some red shoes.* I also remember falling on the sidewalk at the wine shop and the way it felt when he caught my arm. It makes my insides flip over like one of those Slinky toys we played with as kids and I feel myself giggle. I haven't giggled in years. His eyes light up in response.

"I could do that. But…you'll have to catch me if I fall."

And I just might.

The End

Other Books by Mary Flinn...

The One

"Is following your heart worth having it broken?"

"Powerful and timeless, *The One* is a heartwarming story illuminating a love that is, in this age, truly rare. Flinn's depiction of a young woman's ability to remain true to herself in the face of many trials is unrivaled as she powerfully proclaims the importance of faith, family, friendship, and above all, love."

— **Meredith Strandberg, Student,**
North Carolina State University

Second Time's A Charm

"Forgiveness is easy. Trust is harder."

"Mary Flinn is the female equivalent of author Nicholas Sparks. Her characters are as real as sunburn after a long day at the beach. Hot days and hotter nights make *Second Time's a Charm* an excellent sultry romance that will stay with readers long after the sun goes down. The second book in a series, this story is a movie waiting to happen."

— **Laura Wharton, author of *The Pirate's Bastard***
and Leaving Lukens

Three Gifts

"There is a Celtic saying that heaven and earth are only three feet apart, but in the thin places, the distance is even smaller."

"Throughout *Three Gifts*, you will be rooting for Chelsea and Kyle, young marrieds so appealing, yet real that you'll wish you could clone them. They settle in the mountains, near Boone, North Carolina, and when they are faced with tragedies, they handle them with courage and grace. Even those oh-so-human doubts and fears that threaten occasionally to swamp them are banished through humor and the abiding love that sustains them. This is a journey of hope, faith, and love that you'll want to share with them."

— Nancy Gotter Gates, author of the *Tommi Poag* and
Emma Daniel mysteries, and women's fiction
Sand Castles and *Life Studies*

A Forever Man

"There are friends and there are lovers; sometimes the line between is thinly drawn."

"Just when I thought I would never see Kyle and Chelsea Davis again, Mary Flinn brings them back in *A Forever Man*; they returned like old friends you feel comfortable with no matter how much time has passed, only this time with eight-year-old twin boys, and a new set of life-complications to work through. In this novel, Flinn provides a deft look at marriage when potential infidelity threatens it. *A Forever Man* is Flinn's masterpiece to date, and no reader will be disappointed."

— Tyler R. Tichelaar, Ph.D., and author of
Spirit of the North: a paranormal romance

And a stand-alone novel,

apart from the Kyle and Chelsea series:

The Nest

"Are things really meant to be, or are we just sitting around waiting for butterflies?"

"Mary Flinn realistically captures the ideals of an empty nest filled with rekindling passions of soon-to-retire Cherie and her rock-and-roll-loving husband Dave—then flips it all over when Hope, the jilted daughter, returns to the nest to heal her broken heart. Between her mother's comical hot flashes that only women of a certain age could appreciate, the loss of her laid-back father's sales job, and the good news-bad news of other family members' lives, can Hope find the courage to spread her wings and leave the nest again? Flinn's deft handling of story-telling through both Cherie and Hope's voices will send readers on a tremendously satisfying and wild flight back to *The Nest*."

— Laura S. Wharton, author of the award-winning novels
Leaving Lukens, *The Pirate's Bastard*, and others

Author Biography: Mary Flinn

A native of North Carolina, award-winning author Mary Flinn long ago fell in love with her state's mountains and its coast, creating the backdrops for her series of novels, *The One, Second Time's a Charm, Three Gifts, A Forever Man,* and *The Nest.* With degrees from both the University of North Carolina at Greensboro and East Carolina University, Flinn has retired from her first career as a speech pathologist in the NC public schools that began in 1981. Writing a novel had always been a dream for Flinn, who began crafting the pages of *The One,* when her younger daughter left for college at Appalachian State University in 2009. The characters in this book have continued to call to her, wanting more of their story told, which bred the next three books in the series.

Flinn has recently been the recipient of the Reader Views Literary Awards 2012 Reviewers' Choice honorable mention in the romance category for *A Forever Man*. First Place Award for Romance Novel in the Reader Views 2011 Literary Book Awards, as well as the Pacific Book Review Best Romance Novel of 2011 went to *Three Gifts*. *Second Time's a Charm*, also released in 2011, won an Honorable Mention in the Reader Views Reviewers' Choice Awards.

Mary Flinn lives in Summerfield, North Carolina with her husband. They have two adult daughters.

Breaking Out is her sixth novel.